ATLANTIS ENDGAME

ANDRE NORTON & SHERWOOD SMITH

Atlantis Endgame

Copyright © 2002, 2021 Andre Norton and Sherwood Smith
All rights reserved.
This edition published 2021

Cover design by Augusta Scarlett, LLC (www.scarlettebooks.com)

ISBN: 978-1-68068-193-2

The characters and events portrayed in this book are fictitious. Any similarity to real persons, living or dead, is coincidental and not intended by the author.

No part of this book may be reproduced or stored in a retrieval system, or transmitted in any form or by any means, electronic, mechanical, photocopying, recording or otherwise, without express written permission of the publisher.

This book is published on behalf of the authors by the Ethan Ellenberg Literary Agency.

About the authors:
Andre Norton: http://www.andre-norton-books.com/
Sherwood Smith: https://www.sherwoodsmith.net/

ATLANTIS ENDGAME

In Earth's future, when time travel has become possible, the Time Patrol is the top secret government agency that protects Earth's past, so that our history will not become corrupted by invaders from either our future or from other worlds. For many years, Murdock, Ashe, and other members of the Time Patrol have contended with threats to our time continuum, none more deadly than the aliens nicknamed "Baldies", whose distrust of other high-tech civilizations has driven them to a destructive strategy.

In the seventh entry in the Time Traders series, Ross Murdock, Gordon Ashe, and the rest of the Time Patrol travel back to ancient Atlantis.

Evidence of time travel has been found in ruins dating to the ancient world, which is believed to be the legendary realm of Atlantis.

The Time Patrollers deck themselves out as foreign traders to discover that the Baldies are there, their purpose mysterious.

In the meantime, increasing tremors point to imminent apocalyptic cataclysm. But the time agents must remain until they resolve the mystery of the aliens' intent. If they're wrong, it'll be too late... for them and for Earth's future.

Acknowledgments

As always, my thanks to Dave Trowbridge, Tech Wizard of the Redwoods. Also, I would like to thank Diana L. Paxson, who furnished information on oracles of Ancient Greece. Thanks also to Noreen Doyle for data on Ancient Egypt and to Raila Stella Papadopoulou for help with Greek words.

—S. S.

Table of Contents

Chapter One 1
Chapter Two. 9
Chapter Three 17
Chapter Four 29
Chapter Five 39
Chapter Six. 48
Chapter Seven 58
Chapter Eight. 73
Chapter Nine 85
Chapter Ten 96
Chapter Eleven. 106
Chapter Twelve. 111
Chapter Thirteen. 118
Chapter Fourteen. 127
Chapter Fifteen 134
Chapter Sixteen 143
Chapter Seventeen. 150
Chapter Eighteen. 155
Chapter Nineteen 163
Chapter Twenty 172
Chapter Twenty-One 178
Chapter Twenty-Two. 182
Chapter Twenty-Three. 190
Chapter Twenty-Four. 195

Chapter Twenty-Five 200
Chapter Twenty-Six 207
Chapter Twenty-Seven 215
Chapter Twenty-Eight 220
Chapter Twenty-Nine 229
Chapter Thirty 238

About the Authors 247
About the Publisher 249

Chapter One

"Sure we have the new software," Ross Murdock said, scrupulously unaware of his landlady peeping up at him over the tops of her spectacles as she drowned her potted plants for what was probably the fourth time that day. "It's a fine spreadsheet. Plenty of new features."

Gordon Ashe, following him up the stairs inside the hall, looked amused, but said nothing until Ross had shut the apartment door behind him and locked it.

"Nosy landlady, I take it?" Ashe commented.

"The tenants here are better than TV, she seems to think. At least from the gossip she rattles off to Eveleen when she can catch her."

Ashe and Ross both surveyed the plain living room with its garage-sale furnishings. Eveleen had done her best to add homey touches: a brightly colored braided rug on the floor, a few very hardy houseplants, and one or two ancient artifacts brought up from the past—nothing to raise eyebrows, should anyone drop in who knew about such things. But Ross and Eveleen knew the real stories behind them—sometimes even had known the person who had made them, thousands of years before.

Ashe shook his head. "Seems like a lot of trouble to go to, if you ask me. Project Star would be happy enough to issue you living quarters, and the ones married couples get are fairly plush. A lot nicer than this, if you want to know the truth."

"But underground. And it's still there, under their control. I've worked for the Project just about my entire adult life, and I respect everyone in it, but I want my own place. My own space. And so does Eveleen," Ross added.

Ashe opened a hand. "But what happens when you're gone on a mission? It's Project Star that handles your pay and banking, right?"

Ross nodded. "Yeah. They renew our yearly lease when it comes up. They cover the utilities. And they pay the cleaning service that comes through here once a week. Those guys dust and even water the plants." Ross gave the leaves of a spider plant a flick. "So, yeah. They hassle the details, but that's only when we're gone."

Ashe, amused, said, "I confess I don't see the difference. Plus you've got the added annoyance of a nosy landlady."

"But she's not our boss. Maybe it's the street kid in me, but I get itchy at the thought of living under the boss's roof, however benevolent." Ross shrugged, looking sardonic. "Makes no sense, does it?"

"Contrary," Ashe replied. To him, it didn't seem all that long ago when he was assigned the nervy, distrustful troublemaker Ross Murdock, straight from juvenile court. Ross had become one of the best agents in the ultrasecret Project Star in spite—or maybe because—of his readiness to apply action first, and palaver afterward, to unexpected problems.

Ashe dropped down onto one of the chairs, giving Ross a skewed smile. Did the landlady also see the signs of the street kid in him?

Ross brought out a couple of mugs of coffee, giving his old partner an appraising glance. Why was Ashe so silent, staring through the coffee as if he were trying to scry his future in it? Gordon Ashe was a tough, lean man around middle age, sun browned and fit. His blue-eyed gaze was direct and intelligent, his dark hair worn short. His plain brown suit conveyed a semblance of bland city-civilization, but he looked and moved like someone who preferred being out of doors.

To break the lengthening silence, Ross said, "The landlady doesn't seem to believe I'm a computer software salesman."

Ashe blinked and looked up. "I take it you don't think I played a convincing buyer?" he asked, the corners of his mouth deepening.

"Well, neither of us looks much like the TV version of your standard computer geek. In any case, Mrs. Withan thinks I'm a no-account. It's Eveleen she keeps pestering. A 'real lady karate expert'!" His voice went squeaky on the last words, and he clasped his hands and looked skyward. "We can all sleep well of nights, knowing we have a real lady karate expert in the building!"

Ashe laughed, but it was a quick, absent laugh, and Ross sat down on the couch. Yep, something was wrong. Instinct had become conviction. "Well, you didn't come over to shoot the breeze. What's going on?"

Gordon Ashe hesitated, one hand absently touching his breast pocket, where Ross saw the edge of a folded piece of paper. Then Ashe shook his head. "I take it Eveleen is teaching a karate class?"

Ross nodded. "She likes to keep in shape, and it gives her a perfect cover job." He glanced at his watch. "She'll be back in a couple hours."

Ashe struck his hands on his knees and got to his feet again. "You asked what's wrong. There are so many possible levels of wrongness here I don't really know where to begin."

Ross whistled under his breath. *I knew it.* Their last mission—to another planet and thousands of years into its past—had been tough enough, but when Ashe first told them about it he'd been business-as-usual. What could be nasty enough to get the guy—old Ice Veins, some of the younger Time Agents had nicknamed him—this jittery?

"I have a meeting in an hour," Ashe said. "I'd hoped to find both of you here for a strategy powwow first, but maybe it's for the best, because there would be more questions than I could answer."

"All sufficiently mysterious," Ross said, now feeling that inward sense of tension ignite. Incipient action. He could almost smell it, like the ozone moments before a lightning strike.

Ashe paused with his hand out just before Ross opened the door. "Oh, a request," he said, smiling oddly. "When you two do come, would you ask Eveleen to wear those gold earrings of hers?"

"Sure." Ross snorted a laugh. "Going romantic at last?"

Ashe only shook his head again, so Ross opened his front door. There was Mrs. Withan, sweeping the hall stairs.

Ashe sent one of those ironic looks over his shoulder. But after years of playing an astonishing variety of roles, from a Folsom Culture trader to a garbage collector on a planet so far away there was no meaningful measure of distance, he was obviously capable of dealing with one nosy landlady.

"We'll get those statistical disks next round," he said, descending the stairs. "Remember to send me the new catalogues."

"In the mail tomorrow." Ross lifted a hand, watched the landlady's shadow on the opposite wall as she peeped out after Ashe, and then shut the door, laughing softly.

He moved into the kitchen and opened the fridge. Did all newlyweds develop their own codes, almost a private language? He reflected on that as he gathered together the fixings for chicken salad. What Eveleen had begun calling his Threat-o-Meter had gone into the red zone; he strongly suspected that the two of them would be called in early tomorrow. Maybe even tonight. Better get dinner going right away, or they might not get any.

As the meat sizzled in the broiler, he wandered into the bedroom and fired up the computer. Did an e-mail check. That, too, came coded, if it was from Project Star, sufficiently bland messages that even the cleverest hacker—supposing one could actually slip past the Project firewalls—couldn't make anything of. Of course, as to that putative hacker, Ross suspected anyone smart enough to do that had already been hired by Kelgarries.

Nothing on the e-mail.

His Threat-o-Meter ratcheted up another notch.

Evaleen opened the door moments before Ross had everything ready. "Just tossing the salad," he called from the kitchen.

Eveleen appeared in the doorway, small, neat, her mouth quirking just so. "Well, in a minute," he corrected, dropping his utensils and crossing the tiny kitchen so he could grab her up and kiss her.

She returned hug and kiss with surprising strength for so small a woman, but, then, a third-degree black belt in four forms of martial arts is bound to be strong.

"There's trouble," she ventured, after he set her down again.

"How can you tell? I haven't said anything!"

"It's your silence." Her brown eyes narrowed as they studied each other. "And—I don't know, this sense I get." She poked his nose. "Threat-o-Meter?"

"Force nine," he admitted. "Gordon came here, said something mysterious, then took off again without another damn word."

She whistled. "Unlike him, you must admit. Force nine indeed. Let me shower and get something weekendy on. If the call comes tonight, we'll be going out to dinner and a flick." She pointed downstairs.

Ross snorted. "And if Mrs. Withan asks what movie we saw, and what we thought?"

"I read all the reviews of the new ones just yesterday." Eveleen chuckled as she leaned back against his shoulder. "I can handle any questions she might ask. And you just say something grunty and mannish like *I love action flicks* or *Geez, another chick flick.*"

"Grunty and mannish. Check."

Eveleen gave him an unrepentant flicker of a smile, and then her expression went pensive. "I hope you don't hold a grudge against Mrs. W. You have to remember she's the normal one."

"It's normal to nose into everyone's affairs?"

"Well, she takes it to excess, but my point is that she's more normal than we are. Humans do form social and kinship networks. She likes to think of the tenants here as a little social network, a family, and loves to see them all getting together and doing normal things, like big barbecues and July Fourth celebrations with buddies at work and so forth. All the other people in the building seem to know a little about one another, yet here we are, living like a couple of hermits."

"Well, we travel a lot," Ross protested. He added with a grin, "They just won't find out where—or when."

"It's not that; it's us," Eveleen said. "I was thinking about it at the dojo today. They all ask after one another's families and friends, and if someone has a disaster, they rally. Oh, I know if we have problems the Project takes care of us—that's not it. It's just that I realized so many of our social and emotional networks—kinship networks, almost—were formed with people in the past, some on other planets, and we can never get those back. It's finished, because if we go back again in time, we risk ruining the *now*. We can pretend we live with normal people in the here and now, but we aren't really part of the contemporary world; we can't let ourselves be."

Ross took her face in his hands so he could gaze down into those lovely brown eyes flecked with tiny bits of gold. *I could swim in those eyes*, he thought, but that was sensory reaction. What was she thinking? He remembered some of the poetry he'd tried to get out of reading when he was a school kid, proclaiming eyes as the window to the soul. Very poetic, except they weren't. You couldn't really tell what thoughts went on behind those eyes, even the eyes of one you loved more than anything or anybody. "What're we really talking about here?" he murmured. "You want to quit the Project, is that it?"

She shook her head, smiling. "No. Because it really is our family, in a sense, even though we took this apartment to make a kind of grand gesture, as if we really do have a life outside Project Star. But there isn't one. We do have to admit it and not take out our annoyance on innocent busybodies like Mrs. Withan."

Ross kissed her again. "All right. Got it. From now on, I promise to think of Mrs. W. as a normal, *nice* busybody."

Eveleen laughed. "I give up. Lecture over! I'd better grab that shower, or when Gordon's call comes, I'll be not just hungry but grungy."

"Oh! Almost forgot. He said the damndest thing right before he took off. When we do meet up, he wants you to wear your gold earrings. Something dubious about those I don't know?" He wiggled his eyebrows.

"If there is something dubious, no one told me," Eveleen said, going into the bedroom and coming out again with the earrings.

They both looked down at the simple beaten gold hoops on her palms. Inexpensive for golden earrings, a style that women—and sometimes men, according to the vagaries of fashion—had been wearing for thousands of years.

"My dad gave me these when I turned twenty-one," she said. "I don't think that exactly registers as dubious, mysterious, or otherwise provocative."

Ross spread his hands. "Crazy."

Eveleen laid down the earrings, and padded toward the bathroom. "But I guess you never know! Watch 'em in case they suddenly start beeping mystery messages."

"With our luck, they're more likely to explode," he said grimly.

She was still laughing when the phone rang.

Chapter Two

Gordon Ashe reached the restaurant twenty minutes early and was annoyed with himself. He could sit in the bar and brood for what would seem like twenty hours, or he could take his laptop in and look like a pompous fool. Or he could drive around the block twenty times.

With a sigh of annoyance, he got out of his car and tossed the keys to the parking attendant. He checked his watch again, knowing it was a stupid impulse. Thirty whole seconds had sped by!

All right, he was in a sour mood anyway; why not go inside and brood.

The restaurant was an old favorite. It wasn't dark as pitch inside—he hated that—and it had decent food without a lot of the pretentious posturing that seemed to go with it in tonier places. He headed for the bar, which was mostly empty, for the hour was early yet.

A woman sat alone at the end. He almost looked away, but something in the curve of shoulder, the angle of her head zapped his memory. Twenty-five years he hadn't seen her, but he knew her immediately.

"Is that you, Gordon?" Her voice hadn't changed.

"Linnea?" His mind fumbled back and forth between two different tracks of thought: memories of their last meeting—a towering argument—and the e-mail she'd sent him just yesterday. A third track superimposed itself: what subtle measures did the mind use to mark a familiar face or form? He'd probably seen twenty thousand women—more—since he last was in Linnea Edel's presence, but he'd immediately known that precise tilt of chin as if he'd just parted from her an hour ago.

"Yes, it is I," she said, getting off her bar stool and coming forward.

Neither spoke as they looked at each other. *She's the same*, he thought. Oh, older—and she didn't bother to hide it, either. Her thick cloud of dark hair was streaked with gray, and maybe her contours were softer, for she'd never been fashionably thin (or had shown the slightest interest in fashion) back then. She was still short and round, and though age, and experience, and the inevitable effects of gravity had carved lines in her face, her Mediterranean bone structure was more sharply emphasized now, and he realized she was more attractive than ever.

He tried a polite opener. "How was the drive up from New York?"

"Slow. And then pretty." She gave him a rueful smile. "Gordon, I hope you're not mad at me. I realized after you sent your e-mail about meeting here—so neutral a place, like a truce—that maybe it seemed like I was threatening you, and it wasn't that, not at all."

Nothing like the exigencies of work to snap the mind back to the here and now. Aware of interested ears at the bar, Ashe said easily, "Threaten me all you like. I have just as much back history to bore you with as you could have for me. But how about we get a booth first, and we can play catch-up in comfort?"

Her eyes narrowed in a subtle signal of comprehension. She laughed. "Ah, but I came armed with family photos! Lead on."

They were soon settled into a corner booth near the fireplace. A bar waiter appeared, and Ashe asked for seltzer on the rocks with a twist, just to get rid of the guy; he did not want alcohol clouding his brain now. As the waiter moved away, he looked at the drink Linnea had brought and realized she was drinking the same thing.

"Before we start," he said, striving for normalcy, except what is normal when you haven't seen someone since a fight twenty-five years ago, and then she sends you a sinister letter? "Do you really have family photos? How is J.J.? And didn't I hear you'd had kids?"

"Two." She raised her fingers. "Twins. Mariana is in the Navy, doing something arcane with radar, and adores it, when I hear from her, which is about twice a year. Max is in Los Angeles at film school, working about twenty hours a day, which is what you have to do until you break into that business. I hear from him *once* a year."

She had picked up her glass and was gently clinking the ice cubes round and round, round and round. She seemed to realize that she was doing it and set it down again, then tipped her head, that inquiring angle that had reminded him of a bird, and said, "J.J. died five years ago."

"I'm sorry," Ashe said, hating how inadequate it sounded.

"Don't be. It was sudden, over his breakfast coffee. Just like that. I was even there to be with him those last few moments."

Ashe winced.

She laced her fingers together, her wedding band winking with golden light in the reflection from the fire.

"Best way to go, I think. No fear, and the doctors insisted there couldn't have been much suffering. Though it's hard enough on those of us left behind. So I became a hermit for a time, and then that time ended, and I looked about me, and realized that I was still alive, that my children were grown and didn't need me—and that I could, well, have a life of my own."

Again the tilt of the head. "And you were right, by the way."

Right? Was she talking about that last nasty exchange? Ashe's mind wheeled back rapidly, faster than light-speed. He was again on warm, dusty Crete, digging at Knossos. Two on the dig were J.J. Edel, twenty years older, and Linnea, young and earnest and ardent about the archaeology. Gordon swinging between finishing his doctoral work and getting lured by the government into the supersecret Project Star, during the years the Iron Curtain still blocked off the East.

What could he say? He could say—

"Here's your seltzer, sir. Now, are you folks ready to order?"

Ashe accepted the drink, and the waiter launched into a recital of a long list of specials. Ashe took a slug of cold seltzer, fighting the urge to tell the guy to take a hike.

Linnea smiled. "Oh, I'm sorry, we haven't even looked at our menus yet. Would you come back later?"

"Sure. Just wave a hand," the waiter said, and he left.

Linnea leaned forward. "The last time you and I saw one another, if you remember, we were walking along the harbor at Heraklion."

"I remember."

"And you told me, in pungent and specific detail that I can still recall to this day, what a fatheaded doormat I was to do all J.J.'s work at the dig."

Ashe winced and shook his head. "And I've regretted it ever since, though I know that doesn't excuse it."

"Why should you excuse it? You were right. I did do all his work and let him take the credit. A lot of that was the cultural conditioning of the time—that's what ladies did. And you were right about J.J. incidentally: he really wasn't interested in archaeology or in any of the other degrees he almost got. He was just marking time until his father died suddenly and he took over the business, which he ran until the day he died. And I am delighted to say that my son never showed any interest in inheriting it. The new CEO is, in fact, a woman."

Ashe nodded.

"Well, bear with me now, Gordon, because it all ties together." She chuckled softly and again tilted her head. "After you and I had our little talk and you vanished into the ether, J.J. inherited, like I said. And since I was pregnant with the twins—and you know how primitive conditions were at the dig—and J.J. didn't want his little princess working, we both dropped out, moved to New York City, and I became a housewife until the morning I became a widow."

She finished her seltzer and sat back, sighing. "So as I said, my year of being a hermit passed, and then I looked around and realized that I had a life. Not as a mom or a wife, but as me. And I'd always loved archaeology, with a passion. I subscribed all these years to *Archeology* and a half dozen other scholarly magazines. So I decided to go back to school. No hurry and I don't care if I even graduate, because I'd never take one of the rare jobs from some young person struggling to follow his or her dream. J.J. did leave me very well off, so I can do what I want. Which, this last winter, was to go back with some students on a little dig."

She leaned forward, and Ashe did as well. "Not to Crete this time, but to Thera itself. And that's where I found what I sent you."

Ashe now drew the printout from his coat pocket. The picture in itself was nothing of interest to anyone who might glance casually at it: a photo of a hoop earring of beaten gold, somewhat dull, with bits of mud and debris stuck to it, but on the clearest part, quite distinct, was a jeweler's mark. A modern jeweler's mark.

Ashe looked down at it and up at Linnea's face.

She said, "You disappeared that spring from classes, and you kept giving these evasive answers when people asked what you were doing. And a couple of times the department secretary said you got calls from these guys from Washington, DC, which was quite a ways from our university."

Ashe said nothing.

Linnea grinned. "I tried to find you afterward, I have to admit. At first to continue the argument. That comment about doormats did stick in my craw, but as the years went by, and J.J. still called me his little princess, I realized that you were right all along. It stuck because it was true. Oh, I loved him, and he loved me, but J.J. never did see me as an adult in my own right—and I guess the role I got in the habit of playing wasn't exactly conducive to changing his worldview." She waved a hand, as though shooing away an annoying fly. "But we're not here to hash over old feminist issues. The thing is, I did try to find you, as well as some of our old friends, and though I eventually found all of them, you remained amazingly elusive."

She paused, sending Ashe an inquiring look. He said slowly, "Most of my subsequent work was on artifacts here in North America. If you stayed with Aegean studies, of course you'd lose track of me—" He shrugged. He had never minded deflecting people from his real work, but it made him feel queasy to issue these half-lies to a friend.

"Nice try," Linnea said, laughing a little. "I also heard from one of our mutual old friends about a dig in New Mexico, and you'd been in on a find that later vanished. No articles, no papers, no conferences. That, he told me in a letter, spells 'government' and 'top secret.'"

Ashe looked down, fiddling with his drink. What could he say?

She didn't seem to expect him to say anything; she kept on. "Then, a few years back, there was all that news about the alien spaceships, and the tapes, though it all disappeared from the news really quickly when it was discovered that they were old artifacts and aliens weren't coming here in peace or in war. People forgot. But I never did, especially when, it turned out, one of the sites mentioned was New Mexico, and a Dr. Ashe was quoted just once. I put the variables together, wondered if you might be part of the equation, and last winter when I uncovered that earring in a place that had been sealed under volcanic ash since 1628 B.C. and saw that modern jeweler's mark, I decided that maybe it was time to try again to dig you up. Luckily people are easier to find on the Internet these days, even if their jobs aren't."

Ashe let out a sigh. "And you decided to find me because...?"

"I figured if there was anyone who could tell me how a modern earring could get back to the mid-1600s B.C., it was you."

Ashe hesitated. There was one obvious question to be asked, but he didn't think he could bring himself to do it quite yet. So he went to the next obvious. "You were the one who mentioned threats. I take it you haven't shared your find with anyone?"

"And don't plan to, if it will cause trouble. As I said, I am not hunting for a career, or even notoriety. Truth, yes. Insight into the past and how we got here today—the roots of our present civilization—yes. But not at the cost of people's lives. I paid my own way to the dig, so no one owned my time, and if it turns out to be a genuine artifact and I'm wrong, I'll restore it to the Greek government. But I do," she said again, in a low voice, "want to know the truth."

Ashe stared down at the picture again, his mind darting in circles like fireflies in a high wind. Nothing, though, got past that primary question—

"What is it, Gordon?" she whispered. "You look like you'd seen a—oh!" Her voice broke off.

He glanced up, to see her eyes gone round and dark with intensity. He realized he was clammy with sweat. At the same moment he saw a wince of compassion tighten her face, and she murmured in a fast, low voice, "I did not take it from a skeleton. I did not see any remains."

Ashe's breath leaked out, though his heart still hammered.

She gave her head a quick shake. "Of course you know what that dig is like, two more inches, and we don't know what we'll find. But the Marinatos and Doumas teams have not uncovered any human remains so far, and that is still the same."

That leap of compassion, of sudden understanding, was not the reaction of an eager young student desperate to make a mark in the world. It was the reaction of a woman of experience, of integrity. It was the Linnea he'd once known, only grown up.

"I'll see what I can do," he promised.

Chapter Three

Eveleen Riordan felt her gold earrings swing against her jaws as she stepped into the elevator. Why did she feel so self-conscious all of a sudden? How many times had she worn this pair to work and never thought anything of it?

But no one had ever asked about them before. *How odd*, she thought, as Ross tapped a code into the elevator pads. A subtle jerk, a whine of hydraulics, and the elevator did not go up—though the people in the lobby of the Northside Research Institute would think it had. Upstairs a legitimate marketing research company did a thriving business. Down below ground level existed a complex that those busy researchers would have been astonished to discover.

They dropped fast and smooth; then the elevator doors slid open onto spacious hallways with full spread-spectrum lighting and rows of healthy ferns and other plants. Off both sides offices full of computer banks and desk cubicles opened up, people moving to and fro. The designers had made it as pleasant as they could, but to Eveleen it still felt like vintage government-agency ambience, and modest as their apartment was, she was glad to call it home.

"Ah, there you are." Major Kelgarries emerged from an adjacent hallway, three or four disks in one hand and a sheaf of files in the other. *He's been riding a desk for a long time, but he still looks and moves like a man used to being in the field,* Eveleen thought as Ross returned the brief greeting and they followed Kelgarries's broad shoulders the last few paces to one of the conference rooms.

It was one of the big rooms, with a big projection screen on one wall. No one spoke as they entered and set up their laptops. Ross moved straight to the coffee dispenser next to the door and brought them both a cup. Eveleen was still feeling off balance. She smiled at Gordon Ashe, and decided the light touch was the way to handle his odd request. She tapped her earrings and blinked her eyes, as if to say, *See? I remembered!*

He smiled back, but his smile was tight, and perfunctory at best.

Eveleen looked away, troubled, and began seeing the clues she'd overlooked: tension. Tension in Kelgarries, tension in Ashe, tension in Milliard, the big boss, muttering over there into a cell-phone. Tension in the older woman sitting in the corner, laptop open. She talked quietly with the tall redhead whom Eveleen recognized as one of the top computer simulation experts in Project Star.

The redhead gave Eveleen a brief wave.

"Hi, Marilyn," Eveleen murmured. Then wished she hadn't spoken, for her voice seemed oddly loud.

"We're all here," Ashe said then. "Eveleen, if I may trouble you for those earrings, please?"

She no longer felt like laughing as she unfastened and handed them over. In silence she and Ross watched Ashe examine the simple gold loops, then place them on the light-plate of a projecting microscope arranged next to his chair. Eveleen felt Ross tensing up beside her, his gray eyes narrowed.

Everyone watched as Ashe took out a small manila envelope from a file and shook its contents out into his hand: another hoop earring. Then he produced from a pocket a jeweler's eyepiece and bent over the earring, glancing occasionally at the projection screen, where Eveleen's pair loomed as large as basketball hoops, every dimple strike of the jeweler's hammer plain. He reached and turned over the two earrings on the microscope's projection stage.

Eveleen felt tension grip her own neck when she realized she'd heard his breathing stop. In silence he placed the earring from the envelope on the microscope, pushing aside one of the ones already there. There was his hand, big enough for them to see the whorls of his fingerprints as he nudged the earring into the center, next to the other, and then Eveleen realized what she was seeing.

The earring was identical to one of the pair she'd brought, a little more worn, but it had the same little jeweler's squiggle on it and in exactly the same place. It was the same earring.

Cold certainty settled into the pit of her stomach, and Eveleen felt a familiar dizziness; the paradoxical nature of time travel wasn't something anyone ever got used to. She was too experienced a Time Agent to mistake what she and everyone else in the room were seeing: bilocation, the selfsame object existing simultaneously in two places at once.

"Where?" Ross demanded, gazing at Gordon Ashe, his face like granite. "And when? And how long have you known about it?"

Eveleen took her lower lip between her teeth. The truth was, a weird little voice in the back of her mind gibbered and giggled, Mrs. Withan was *scared* of Ross. He had no idea he looked as out of place in her clean, low-key apartment building as a pirate in a swimming pool. Tall, lean, scarred hand, his walk the silent, action-ready walk of someone who was raised on the streets, Ross didn't look even remotely like any sort of software salesman.

The street kid was very obvious in his attitude now. But Ashe had been handling that oblique threat for years.

"To answer your questions in reverse order: I did not know about it until last night. 'When' is somewhere in the middle of the 1600s B.C. We think it might be 1628. And where..." He smiled wryly. "Have you ever heard of the legend of Atlantis?"

Eveleen said, startled, "But that's New Age woo-woo!"

Ross then surprised her—surprised everyone—by saying, "Plato, fourth century B.C. Retelling Solon's story."

Kelgarries snorted a mirthless laugh. "Glad I didn't put any bets on that one."

Gordon nodded, giving Ross a brief smile. "Dialogues between Timaeus and Critias. So you did a little reading while you were up at my cottage in Maine?"

Ross grinned back. "Books were on the shelf, and you did say to feel free."

Gordon looked around at them all. "Our so-called Atlantis, as far as we can tell, did in fact exist. But it was not a great continent, and it did not sink. It was a volcanic island—actually an arc of small islands, the very top of a massive undersea volcano—just north of Crete, now called Thera. Which means 'fear'," Gordon added with a sardonic lift of his brows. "The people of the time seem to have called it Kalliste. And as near as we can tell, approximately in the 1620s B.C. from thirty to fifty cubic miles of it blew into the sky, sending out a tsunami that took out all the ports along the Aegean and sent a black cloud into the atmosphere that ruined crops in China and showed up in tree rings as far away as northern California."

Eveleen rubbed her temples, stunned at what had to have been the magnitude of that volcanic eruption.

Kelgarries turned to the red-haired expert. "Marilyn?"

"For purposes of comparison," she said in a strong French accent, "the explosion at Mount St. Helens in Washington was an explosion of a mere half-cubic-mile, as you Americans would say. Krakatoa was about eight cubic miles."

The woman next to her—short, thick graying hair—listened, taking notes steadily, but as yet she had not spoken, and no one had introduced her.

Ashe tapped the projection stage of the microscope, making the huge images on the screen tremble and bringing their attention back to the earrings. "And this was discovered buried under approximately twenty-five meters—say eighty feet of volcanic ash, undisturbed until just this summer."

Ross looked sick. "A volcanic island?" His mouth tightened. "I suppose our bones were next to it?"

Eveleen felt her heart squeeze at that *our*. No one had mentioned him yet, but she knew that he'd be there beside her, somehow, no matter how.

"No," Ashe said. "Understand that the progress at that dig is barely measured in inches, especially in the past few years, and as yet there have been no remains. Just a few scattered artifacts in the street of a city. The people, as far as we can tell, seem to have been evacuated."

"By us?" Eveleen spoke, her throat dry. That voice at the back of her mind was no longer laughing. *If everyone got away, why was my earring there?* "I mean, it's clear that we were there. That we're going to be there."

Ross tapped a pencil on the edge of his laptop, a militant tattoo. "Why all this background chat? Are you building up to some big idea about the Baldies maybe causing that volcano to blow?"

"Well, we don't know," Ashe said. "The truth is, until yesterday somehow this remarkable incident in Earth's history had seemed a random natural event, albeit extraordinarily spectacular. As a possible site for our investigations, it had been previously overlooked. Probably because as yet there has been so little excavation done, and we know so very little about what happened—and of course there had been no mysterious artifacts found, none of the globe ships or other signs of the Baldies that we've discovered and dealt with in other times and places."

Eveleen's mind worked rapidly through what she knew of history. "Thera...north of Crete. Those were the Minoans, weren't they? The bull worshippers? Weren't they supposed to be this sophisticated, peaceful trading civilization?"

"They were," Ashe said. "They were probably the most sophisticated culture Earth had produced until the past couple of centuries—and some will argue about that, considering the wars we've managed to wage against ourselves and the environmental damage our industrial developments have caused. The Minoan houses that have been excavated so far had running water, possibly hot and cold. Toilets. Showers, even, in one place. A standard of living, in short, that would not be out of place today. Only they didn't wage war, they traded, all along the Mediterranean, for their distinctive artwork shows up in tombs in Egypt as well as points north and west. Yet right around this time they vanished. Simply disappeared from history."

Ross nodded. "Right. But you said that no bodies were found, and that they might have evacuated. So how did that civilization vanish?"

"No one knows," Milliard said, pointing to a sheaf of printouts. "We've pulled up as much research as we can, and most of it is speculation."

Eveleen looked around. Anomalies—events that could have been caused by outside agency—existed all through the human past, of course. She and the other Time Agents had certainly experienced enough outside interference from the hairless, humanoid aliens they called Baldies to make every incident that did not have clear cause and effect appear suspicious.

Ross frowned. "What we might be looking at here is some kind of dirty work, then? Someone deliberately setting back the development of our civilization a couple thousand years?"

Ashe pressed his thumbs into his eye sockets. "It is one hypothesis, isn't it? Marilyn and her team have been up all night running sims on this, and correlating it with what we know. The most accepted hypothesis in my field posits that if the Minoans had survived, we might have had our industrial revolution at least a thousand years ago—if not more. We might be immortal by now. Colonies on other planets. But though theories are neat, as is usual when dealing with human psychology, it might not be that simple."

Kelgarries said, "There's apparently even a computer analog in Athens, made some two thousand years ago." And he looked over at the gray-haired woman. "Mrs. Edel? What was that you were telling me about earlier?"

The woman spoke for the first time. "It's called the Antikythera mechanism. It was pulled off a shipwreck. Layers of interlocking gears, with readouts to calculate and display astronomical positions." As she spoke her eyes widened with just that sort of wonder that sometimes characterized Gordon Ashe when he talked about the mysteries of the past. *The eternal curiosity of the scholar,* Eveleen thought.

And Milliard said, "Mrs. Edel is our authority on the time and culture."

The woman gave them a tentative smile. Eveleen met her dark gaze, with its expression of inquiry, and smiled back.

Ross also gave the woman a nod and smile, but it was a distracted smile. He was back tapping his pencil again, his scarred fingers tense. "A computer, eh? So, what, we're going back to see if the Baldies dropped a couple of their equivalent of nuclear bombs down the shaft of that volcano?" He sat back and sighed. "But if they caused the volcano to blow, then it doesn't really matter if it was them or Mother Nature, does it? It already happened. That means if we were there we lost the battle, and it happened. If we'd been successful—if we were to be successful in stopping 'em—then we might destroy ourselves up at this end of time."

"Yes, and no," Ashe said, leaning forward. "As usual, it's not that simple; it's not clear that the Baldies touched off the volcanic explosion by some arcane means." He turned to the computer expert. "Marilyn?"

"There is another hypothesis that projects an unexpected version of what our modern times might have been like if the Minoans had lived," she said, tapping at her computer console.

The light under Ashe's display blinked out, and the power shifted.

Once again the screen came to life, this time with a picture of the Mediterranean world. "This hypothesis, less popular, begins with the obvious statement that our present-day civilization is a direct result of that disaster."

Eveleen frowned, staring at the map.

"The key word, now, is *peaceful*," Marilyn went on. "The Minoans were peaceful and stable. If they had continued to build their remarkable ships and carry goods and ideas around the world, there is a chance we would have developed along more peaceful lines. Most of our technological development has been a side effect of inventions for warfare. Or defense. This second model gives us this picture—" The image shifted. "Had the Minoans continued to influence our development, Earth's population would have grown slowly, engaged more in trade than warfare, giving us—today—a largely pastoral civilization of maybe half a billion people."

The images showed humans in small towns amid great forests and swathes of undisturbed land.

"Our state of technological advance might be the equivalent of the early steam age."

Kelgarries said, "Which would leave Earth open for invasion."

Eveleen sat back in surprise. "So what you're saying is that the Baldies—if they were there at all—might have gone back, or might go back, to *prevent* the volcano from going off?"

"It's possible," Ashe said. "In which case none of us would exist."

Eveleen shut her eyes, struggling—as she always did—with the idea of time and what the higher-math experts termed *superpositions*. *After all I've been through, you'd think I could get used to thinking in the conditional, nonrelativistic tenses,* she thought wryly. And she noticed Ross rubbing his forehead; he was having just the same trouble.

"The key thing to remember is that we seem to have gone back," Ashe said. He added with a faint, sardonic smile, "I say 'we' even though all we have is Eveleen's earring. But I know Ross won't be kept from going on this mission—"

"Damn straight."

"And I confess I would pull any strings I had to pull to be there as well."

Ross flipped his pencil into the air. "All right, so what we're looking at is a trip to the past. See if we find any Baldies. If we don't, we come back. If we do, then what?"

"Circumvent them, of course," Eveleen said.

Ashe nodded at her. "If they did tamper with Thera's volcano, we have to find out what they intend. We might also be the ones who caused the evacuation—"

"Oh, yes," Eveleen exclaimed. "I was just thinking of that. Those people have no other way of knowing, do they? So do you think we are the ones who got them safely away?"

"We won't know anything until we get there," Ashe said. "And we'll begin training at once; we will have to assume that time is pressing."

"Why?" Linnea Edel asked, leaning forward. "If we can truly travel back to any time—a concept I still have trouble grasping, even with the evidence before my eyes—why can't we just take a few months—years, even—to prepare and go back at our leisure?"

Gordon Ashe indicated the three earrings. "To put it simply, the anomaly of this earring being here twice might be something the Baldies can vector in on. We don't want to find out if your discovering that earring, and our bringing it here to its original self, has triggered some kind of detector; the sooner we go back to 1628 B.C. the better."

"So who is going?" Ross asked, hands on his knees.

Kelgarries said, "You, and our top two Greek Time Agents. Stavros Lemkis is down in the labs experimenting with some of the technology you brought back from your previous mission." He nodded at Ross. "Konstantin Skrumbos, our maritime expert on that time, is flying back from the Aegean right now, so he can join the briefing sessions."

Eveleen felt a surge of excitement. Few women agents went into human prehistory because so few cultures had permitted women to move about. But the Minoans had been different.

Milliard got to his feet. "Jonathan?"

A youngish man stepped forward. He looked tired. Eveleen felt a surge of compassion; had he been up for days and nights? But tiredness wouldn't explain that painful quirk to his underlids, the lines beside his mouth. This man was deeply unhappy.

"As yet," Jonathan said, "no one has established what language the people of Kalliste spoke. Linear B has proved to be an Ancient Greek form, but those tablets date from a later time. The few written artifacts from our time are written in hieroglyphs we call Linear A, which have recently been recorded. They, too, proved to be a kind of proto-Greek, but we have very few words in that language—not enough for your communication needs."

He paused to look around. "There are many archaeologists who still feel that the Kallistans first came over from Anatolia, that they are Hittites or Luvians, or even Amorites, bringing the bull worship with them, though it developed into a much more peaceful form. We've put together a core vocabulary that might enable you to understand some words, or at least to begin to form a vocabulary. You will pose as traders, say from Egypt, and we'll give you some Ancient Egyptian language training as well as some Ancient Greek, since traders in that area did get all around the eastern Mediterranean."

Milliard frowned. "The thing to keep in mind—never lose sight of—is the fact that in this situation, we know, or think we know, the year the volcano exploded, but we don't know the day. So we'll put you where we think you're safe, but you'll have to act fast. There's no time to be digging in and doing linguistic studies, no matter how tempting they might be." He cast a meaningful glance Ashe's way, but Eveleen wondered if the warning was actually for Mrs. Edel, who had been listening with intense focus.

"Yes," Ross said, his wary expression back. "Fast. I like fast."

"Marilyn can show you the sim on what happens when the volcano goes off, based on evidence from St. Pierre early in the twentieth century, and Krakatoa, and St. Helens. It's fairly grim," he said.

No one spoke; Eveleen saw Linnea Edel looking down at tightly gripped hands.

Kelgarries spoke up, looking tense and tired and very serious, "What we can be sure of is that nothing within a hundred miles of the blast—whatever day it occurred on—could have lived through it."

Chapter Four

The Aegean sky was mild as milk, a pale, hazy blue with gauzy brush strokes of high cirrus that reminded Ross of southern California. The cargo vessel now plowing its way through the choppy seas could have been heading for Catalina Island. Strange, how you expect the cradle of civilization to be exotic, to strike the senses with profound or dramatic impact. Not like familiar territory.

"Look there. Just off to the northwest," Gordon Ashe said, coming down one of the steel ladders and pointing off the starboard bow.

Ross turned his attention briefly seaward. Just past a smaller craft, equally nondescript, he saw bumps on the horizon. He heard clunking and clanging on the steel ladder from the bridge. Down came Eveleen and Linnea Edel, the latter with more care. All of them had field glasses. Ross pulled up his own pair and shaded the sun with one hand while he focused with the other.

Thera, at this distance, even looked a little like Catalina. He envisioned yesterday's flyover: an island cluster looking like a half-submerged donut. The center, now a peaceful lagoon, with brilliant clear water and a couple of islands dotting it, was the sleeping caldera of the mighty volcano that had blasted fifty cubic miles of matter into the sky.

Everyone studied it in silence as the cargo ship made its way in a slow circle all round the island cluster. Behind them, glimpsed earlier that morning, lay Crete, a long, thin blade of an island. Way off to the northwest, behind Thera, lay more of the Greek islands, and finally Greece itself. To the northeast lay what was once ancient Anatolia, Turkey now.

Getting a basic familiarity with the island and its surroundings now would save them a lot of time when the beautiful little craft lying shrouded in the cargo vessel's hold was launched through the great time-gate two nights hence. They wouldn't, of course, limit themselves to seventeenth-century B.C.E. technology: the ship had a small, virtually silent engine concealed in its stern, but it was only for emergencies. And there'd certainly be no GPS satellites to lock onto, so they'd be navigating using techniques that differed very little from those of the mariners of that period. Best, as always, to go in with as much information as possible, even though there was no way of knowing just how much the surrounding sea and islands had been changed by the volcanic explosion.

It was hard to imagine this peaceful, sunny scene vanishing under a fireball of steam and vaporized rock, then choking under a pall of volcanic ash as glowing volcanic rock fell like hellish hail. Ross shook his head. He knew the reality was the huge magma dome deep underneath the island, just welling up, shouldering aside the rock around it.... Somehow going up against a volcano seemed tougher than facing aliens with laser weapons. You can't even pretend to negotiate with a volcano.

He felt a nudge against his arm, and saw Eveleen at his shoulder, silently studying the biggest island. They were close enough to see striated rock, compressed levels of pumice and ash angling up, indicating tectonic activity no less powerful—only slower.

"I don't care what that lady finds," Ross muttered, glancing over at Linnea Edel. "In and out."

Eveleen grunted in agreement. "What bothers me is that they don't have dates for the Big Blow. It's educated guesswork, but still guesswork."

"I don't mind being put in there a year in advance," Ross said. "I don't want to jet through the gate to find ourselves in the middle of the eruption."

"No." Ashe appeared on Ross's other side, silent of step. "None of us does." He looked amused.

Ross figured he'd complained enough, so he didn't respond. The truth was, he flat-out did not like this mission. There were too many variables. On the surface it looked easy: go in, see if the Baldies are around, and if they are, find out what they're up to. But in Ross's experience, the "easy ones" were the ones that always went screwy. Usually that just meant they had to use their wits, and maybe their fists. But how do you use either against a volcanic eruption?

He said nothing, though, as the cargo ship angled round the western portion of the island and steamed north.

When they had completed their circuit, the team descended aft to the wardroom, which had been made over into a command post. Maps had been pinned up against bulkheads, with labels in English and Cyrillic: the Russians in the other ship were due to come over for the last planning session, over dinner. Stavros and Konstantin were already there.

Ross and Eveleen had just gotten fresh coffee and were sitting down when the ship gave a lurch and muffled clanks and metallic groans announced the skiff grappled alongside.

A short time later three Russians ducked through the hatchway. Without a word the ship's steward handed out the dark Russian tea they all favored, in the little glass cups held in wire frames.

The Russians, two men and a woman, sat down, and Ashe took over to run again through the familiar drill. Too familiar. Ross knew he should pay attention. This launch through the biggest time-gate ever made—stretched between two ships—was a first for both the Russians and Americans. There were too many firsts here, but none of them concerned Ross. Stavros and Konstantin, who would remain aboard their craft, would masquerade as Kallistan sailors. They were actually in charge of the time-gates. Ross couldn't do anything about that, so he scowled down at his coffee. The mission wasn't really real yet, in a sense. Wouldn't be until he and Eveleen went to their cabin for the last time, and pulled on those costumes waiting there.

And she put on those earrings, one of which was lost for over three thousand years.

Eveleen stood with her feet apart, rolling unconsciously with the ship, as she stared down at the earrings in her hand. She had never been much of a philosophic type. Action was what she liked and understood. But you can't help picking up ideas as you go through life, and she remembered someone or other talking once about the single flap of a butterfly's wings causing a forest halfway around the world to fall a hundred years later.

How can one ever know for certain which of our movements causes disaster? Well, she wasn't about to test that theory now. She knew that one of these earrings would, somehow, end up on that island. Where its mate would go—where *she* would go—was what she had to discover.

But she wouldn't risk doing damage to history by leaving those earrings behind. Or leaving one behind, and tossing the other one onto a road in Akrotiri on their arrival.

She sighed and put the earrings in her ears, then turned around to find Ross watching her. His gray eyes were wide, and wary, but he didn't say anything other than "Let's get it over with."

Together they exited the cabin, leaving behind all their obvious twenty-first-century trappings: watches, rings, running shoes, machine-stitched synthetic fabrics. Their equipment had all been cleverly disguised.

Eveleen wore a flouncy three-tiered skirt and a short jacket with embroidery along the outer arms and down the sides. Under it she wore a thin cotton garment. Ross wore a brightly colored kilt of mostly red and black cloth, his skin dyed a deep brown with a long-term sunscreen worked into the chemical makeup of the dye. His black hair, which he had been growing, had been crimped and permed into tight curls, which he held back from his face with a thin gold headband. Both of them wore sandals that tied up their calves.

They met Ashe and Linnea Edel down in the hold. Eveleen was startled to see how different they both looked. Of course Ashe was good at taking on attributes of whatever culture he chose to adopt, and now he appeared to be a trader, his blue eyes hidden behind brown contact lenses.

Linnea Edel, however, had loosened her curly hair, and dressed in the flowing garments of a Kallistan. She looked so like a Greek woman she could have stepped from one of the beautiful painted pots or wall frescoes.

Their two Greek agents, Stavros and Konstantin, had donned the plain linen kilts and sandals of sailors of the time. Konstantin looked like a Greek pirate. Stavros, though superficially resembling Konstantin in his brown skin, dark eyes, and curling hair, was thinner, wirier, and he wore the indefinable air of the engineer.

Both of them were waiting beside the beautifully crafted little boat that would be their trading vessel. Its simple lines concealed an amazing concentration of equipment, including, fastened along the bottom, a small undersea sled for scuba exploration.

"Everyone in," Ashe said, waving his hand.

They climbed in, Stavros and Konstantin going down into the hold where the electronics that would synchronize them with the time-gate were hidden.

Linnea Edel looked around, ran her hands up her arms. With a pang of compassion, Eveleen saw that the skin along her arms was rough with goose bumps. She was frightened; that was easy enough to see.

"I think I'll ride this one out below," Linnea said with a faint smile.

Ashe nodded once, and the older woman vanished below as well, to seat herself among the carefully aged wooden barrels that would, if the mission were extraordinarily lucky, return full of volcanic test materials and various Theran goods—

Kallistan goods, *Eveleen thought, correcting herself.* The island is now Kalliste.

Kallistan goods for the scientific brains back home to happily pore over.

"You two going below?" Ashe asked. Eveleen couldn't quite get used to his gaze, suddenly so dark. Even though she knew that the effect was just caused by lenses, they still gave him a faintly sinister air.

Ross shook his head once. "Want to see."

There was no enjoyment in his tone. Eveleen knew that Ross, in fact, hated the translation between one time and another as much as she did. It was too easy, when one saw that glaring light, and smelled the energy-tortured air, to believe that humans were never meant to endure that wrench.

But endure it they would. The Russians had lost an entire base in the Baltic through a misunderstanding of how the big portals worked. They insisted they had mastered it, and supposedly here was the proof.

Eveleen thought, as the cargo bay doors began to widen, that if anything went awry, hopefully they would never know what hit them.

"Sit toward the center," Stavros said in heavily accented English.

"Speak Ancient Greek," Ashe corrected, using the Greek of Linear B, so painfully decoded just within the past twenty-five years.

Why is he being dogmatic? Eveleen thought, looking Gordon's way. Then she thought back to the hasty training, the many sessions prefaced with "As you've already learned," and "As you well know..."

They did know. That is, all of them except Linnea. Just the day before Kelgarries had taken Ross and Eveleen aside and said, "Your archaeological expert is a first-class academic, and you can rely on her for information. But she only sat through training tapes. There wasn't time for anything else. Watch out for her."

Eveleen sighed. Of course they would watch out for one another. And, so Linnea Edel hadn't had the full course of training? Neither had Ross, once upon a time. And Linnea seemed a lot more sensible than a very young Ross probably had been.

At the inward image of a very young, and impetuous, Ross, she grinned. Stavros flashed her a smile, raised a hand, and then restated in the language they'd all been drilling as hard as they could, day and night: "Sit along the keel."

Ashe, Eveleen and Ross settled along the benches running down the middle of the narrow deck, under a very plain awning. The great engines of the cargo ship thrummed through the wood of the boat, making Eveleen's bones thrum in vibration.

The boat slid, at first slowly, then faster and faster down a ramp, until it shot out onto the choppy waters of the Aegean, reflecting lights from the three ships now steaming in an exact parallel.

Water sprayed up, cooling their faces with shocking suddenness. The boat shuddered and wallowed, and Eveleen clasped her hands tightly together, determined to show no nervousness. She so much preferred to be taking action herself, but this was not part of her job: she could do nothing.

As she forced herself into the steady breathing she'd made second nature during her long studies in martial arts, the boat settled into the rhythm of the waves. Stavros and Konstantin efficiently deployed the single sail, and then sheeted it home.

Now the little boat came alive, lifting the prow up and over the waves. The wind was little more than a gentle breeze, but these shallow craft had been designed for the trickish zephyrs of the Mediterranean climate, and the cargo ship fell away with surprising speed behind them, until it was just running lights against the black horizon.

Eveleen tipped her head back and looked up at the full moon, the Pleiades stretched across the sky like a broken necklace.

The two Russian ships ahead on either side were black silhouettes against a sky barely lit by a gibbous moon. Then a sheath of blue light flickered over their hulls. The air seemed to tighten, and Eveleen thought she heard, deep below the range of human hearing, a vast bell toll, rolling like an irresistible tide through her body. Ahead the sea glowed, a line of bluish light drawn through the chop between the two ships. She heard the slap of flying fish on either side of their small craft as sea life fled the sudden tension in the fabric of the world. Now light billowed up from the sea, diaphanous waves of mist, like a sea-level aurora.

The ship surged forward as a wind began to blow toward the gates, and as the glowing mist surrounded them, Eveleen's skin prickled, but not from the power being deployed around them to wrench a 3,600-year-deep hole in the universe. There were shapes in the mist, wraiths moving, reaching, supplicating, fleeing her direct glance and seen only in the corner of her vision. No one spoke, but everyone was alert and scarcely breathing.

Stavros reached down, pushing on something in one of the storage chests on either side of the keel. The water around their craft suddenly boiled without heat as the series of portal rods carefully spaced along both sides of the ship pulled power from the field now building between the Russian ships. A faint, keening note of power leashed to an extreme degree made Eveleen grit her teeth as the mist began to flow inward toward a bright point of light. It was not a vortex, but straight lines converging on an infinity that flowed hungrily forward to engulf the boat, as though her blind spot was expanding to fill her vision. She saw the prow vanish, wrenched away in a direction her eyes couldn't follow; then nothingness slid forward toward the group huddled in the middle of the boat. There was now no sense of motion, only a sense of a physical violation so great it made nausea seem pleasure by comparison. It seemed endless—

But only for a moment. Her blind spot filled the world and dwindled behind her, giving her for a moment the feeling of eyes in the back of her head, and they were through, sailing into ancient waters.

Chapter Five

The first thing to hit Ross was the acrid odor. No smoggy New York day smelled as bad as this. His hindbrain gibbered with warning at that invidious, pervasive whiff of smoke and the stench of brimstone.

There was no fire, of course. But on previous missions, when Ross transferred into human prehistory, one of the first things he noted was how the stars in the night sky were astonishingly bright: clearer, much clearer, than the clearest night in his own time. This time they were just as faint as the stars over New York City, but there was no kilowattage of civilization to blame.

The haze was volcanic ash.

When are we, exactly? he thought. And then shrugged. Useless to think in terms of exact correlation between dates. When they returned up-time, they'd emerge from the gates whenever they were next energized—probably only moments after they'd entered, no matter how long they spent here. What mattered was when they were in relation to the day of the eruption. That had been the computer jockeys' job. If they hadn't done it right, if there wasn't enough time to make sure the volcanic explosion happened, there'd be no second chance, for a kind of exclusion principle governed time travel: their presence here excluded their earlier presence. Research, and bitter experience, had shown that only inanimate objects could bilocate, like Eveleen's earring.

Sentient beings could not. If they tried to jump up-time and then back here again to gain more time to figure things out, the boat would arrive intact but empty of life, like the *Marie Celeste*, the famous half-brig that'd run afoul of the natural time-fold in the Bermuda Triangle. Seventy years later, that story, and others like it, had inspired the research that led to time travel. Had led to Ross and Eveleen, and the other agents, being here, days? weeks? away from an explosion of unimaginable magnitude. He wondered briefly what happened to that crew, then dismissed the thought. If they didn't succeed here, there'd never be a *Marie Celeste*, and...No time for that. He wrenched his thoughts away before he got a headache, feeling a grin twitch at his lips at the inadvertent double meaning of "time."

Almost at once Ross turned his head from the silent stars to the hatch to the below-deck area, where golden light glowed.

Stavros had jumped down as soon as they were through. He popped up now. "We came through fine," he said, in the Ancient Greek they must all speak now.

Ross felt Eveleen relax beside him. He said nothing, of course. She'd hate him noticing. He also saw Ashe's grim profile ease slightly.

"Good," Ashe said, as though aware of attention turning his way. "It is night in both worlds. Much to do on the morrow. Let's get some sleep while we can."

They nodded, and trooped below, ducking under the narrow roof. Hammocks woven of net had been provided, and they had all practiced sleeping in them. Ross climbed into his, aware of the breathing of the others, and the balmy air that was just this side of being stuffy and too warm. The day would be blistering, unfortunately. No help for that. Air conditioning was now three thousand years in the future.

The steady lap-lap of the water along the sides, and the gentle rocking, sent him into a deep sleep that only broke when he heard voices.

It wasn't just the voices of his team, either, he realized. Bright sunlight shafted down into the crowded hold, golden rays that fired thousands of dust motes.

On deck was comparative silence; the voices came from beyond the ship. Ross looked around, realized he was alone.

He tumbled out of his hammock and ran up the short ladder to find Eveleen, Ashe, and Linnea gathered under the awning, eating some bread from the stores Stavros and Konstantin had stashed below. Stavros worked as helmsman with a great paddled tiller; Konstantin tended the sail.

The air was hot, still, and hazy with faint smoke. It made the brightness into a fierce glare. Ross squinted against the fierce light, shading his hand against the splashes of fiery sun on the harbor waters.

They had reached Akrotiri, he realized. They were in the midst of what seemed to be hundreds of craft, all more or less like theirs: high of prow, low aft, narrow, and built for speed over relatively mild waters. The main characteristic of one set of boats was the single square sail on a mast. Some of those sails were made of what looked like rough-woven linen, others of matting; the masts varied from single pieces rough-carved from trees to poles lashed together. These little boats would never last an hour in an Atlantic storm, but they were fast to make and easy to sail in the Mediterranean and Aegean waters.

Most of those with the masts were hauling their wind, drifting southward and away.

Eveleen gasped. "Have we arrived just at the departure of the fleet?" she murmured, staring.

Ross heard Linnea respond in a low voice, "Departure of *a* fleet, perhaps. I do not believe the entire island vacated overnight."

The other boats, the ones remaining in the harbor, were an astonishing variety. Some were long and narrow, with twenty and more rowers on each side. A few were so low that the rowers sat, visible, working with the sun broiling their dark heads and bronzed necks. Others had the galley slaves hidden below, in decks probably hot and noisome but at least out of the sun.

Most of the craft had no sails; they were local transportation. And a great many of them were spectacularly painted along the sides, with figures of birds, dolphins, even lions, and the awnings above the passengers were decorated with crocuses and lilies.

At first no one from these bravely decorated boats gave their own plain, modest craft a second glance.

The crowd of voices resolved into individuals. Ross, listening closely, was somewhat relieved to hear a mix of languages: there was Ancient Egyptian and Ancient Greek as well as one that was incomprehensible. People seemed to switch back and forth between tongues, calling greetings, complaining about the heat, demanding space to unload goods, starting in on trade negotiations. Requesting news of friends and relations since the "rock rain." Exchanging gossip. Human relations, in short, exactly like those of their unknown descendants thousands of years up the time-line.

"Rock rain," Linnea Edel repeated, staring out intently. Ross watched the woman continually turning her head, scanning, listening, and figured she probably would give an arm or a leg for a tape recorder, if not a video cam.

Rock rain: one of the falls of pumice that the scientists had talked about, resulting from a preliminary eruption.

Ross felt a pang of trepidation inside. The science brains had guessed pretty close, then.

Eveleen sat on the railing, earrings swinging, as she watched a low-lying fishing smack ease up to the beach. No one looked her way as she observed the crew splash overboard, anchoring the ship with net-bound rocks on either side and then beginning unloading.

Ross looked about. The crew of the fishing boat seemed to be mostly comprised of men, but not completely. Lithe young girls in their teens and maybe a bit older scrambled about in some of the fishing boats, obviously experienced at their work.

"Yah!" An insistent shout, followed by a quick stream of words, brought all their attention around.

Eveleen exchanged looks with Linnea Edel, who leaned forward, as if to take notes.

Damn it anyway, were they already to be exposed?

Ross turned, to see a man about his own age standing with one foot propped on the side of his boat, calling through cupped hands. An official of some sort, something they couldn't plan for?

But before Ross could say anything, the man switched to Ancient Egyptian of his own accord, and cried, "You there. What are you carrying?" His accent was strange, not at all like that of Jonathan and his team. Slurry, too quick. But Ross had encountered that syndrome before: language was always slower and more tentative in the lab. Here, it was real, living communication.

He mentally framed his response, then said: "Marble and a few other items."

"Then why are you here, where the foods are landed and brought to market?"

"It is our first journey to Kalliste."

"Ah. I thought you were Kemtiu." *Kemtiu*—the word the Egyptians used for themselves.

"Yes."

"There is always place for Kemtiu," the man called, and he bent down to talk to someone below his deck, and then straightened up. "And marble. Just as long as you bear no fruits."

So this man was just nosing out the competition.

"Our only food is for here," Ross said, striking his stomach.

The man laughed, and Ross laughed with him, then said, "Where is the best warehouse for us to unload our goods?"

"You'll want to sail down to that warehouse there with the dolphins painted on the side. We only have two left standing. Temo here is cousin to the owner and says he is honest enough, and speaks Kemt."

"We shall do so. Thank you, and may the gods smile on you."

"And on you." The two boats parted.

The setup made sense: perishables would be unloaded closest to Akrotiri and the market. Other things could be brought by cart.

Stav and Kosta expertly turned the boat, angling parallel to the coast. They made their way through the tangle of craft, sailing parallel to the shore.

Ross and the others studied the buildings dotting the mountainside. And it was a mountain, too, he realized, squinting against the bright haze. Present-day Thera had high cliffs, but here those cliffs were a small part of a sizable mountain, the top of which was obscured in a grayish-brown cloud of smoke. Much of the lower slopes looked adrift with something resembling dirty snow.

"Looks quite threatening, doesn't it?" Linnea Edel murmured, staring up.

"But no one else seems to notice," Eveleen replied.

"It's business as usual for these particular Kallistans," Ashe said. "And so should it be for us as well," he added with meaning.

The rest took the hint, and began to busy themselves about the little ship as Stavros and Konstantin, at yard and tiller, respectively, angled the boat toward a bare patch of beach near great buildings with tiled roofs. One had sun-faded dolphins painted on one wall. Konstantin lowered the sail and vanished below, and then the two men let out the heavy anchors with a splash.

The water was quite shallow, but so were the boats. Ross jumped overboard, turning to extend a hand to Linnea. They waited for the slight surge of water to diminish, and then she jumped in, her hem getting wet. The water was warm, though, Ross noted as they waded ashore.

For a time they all remained busy, as Stav and Kosta negotiated with the warehouse owner for space, and then hired harbor laborers to unload the pieces of pink and salmon and golden marble that the science techs back home had determined would be appropriate trade items from Egypt. They also unloaded the linen bolts that the women would use as trade samples in order to talk to any local merchants they might find.

Then they all oriented themselves, noting where the boat was anchored with reference to the harbor. If necessary they had radio contact, but they wanted to use it as little as possible. The Kallistans would never notice, but what was sent out via EM might be intercepted by other high-tech listeners—like the Baldies.

Ashe was the last to step onto the pumice-spattered white sands. He opened his mouth to speak, but then paused, his brow puckered.

Ross realized the ground was still undulating beneath his feet. An effect of just getting off the water?

Before his mind could frame the question, other sensory details sparked his sense of danger: an explosion of swallows skyrocketing upward, scolding; the rumble of stone grating in walls and buildings of the city just half a mile away.

Earthquake!

The Time Agents all looked up, hands out. Ross realized he was safest right where he was, out in the open. Somewhere in the harbor city, just right of the great gates next to which sacred horns trembled, a sudden white cloud of dust shot upward: either a wall, or a building, had collapsed.

But the city did not change. Far too many of the great buildings, some three stories, had already fallen some time ago. The people who had not evacuated the city appeared to have moved into the smaller buildings, patching them in makeshift ways and carrying on with business as usual. The only damage that the Time Agents could see was bits of carvings falling to the streets below and smashing a row of hanging plants that had been set along a roof edge.

Before anyone could speak, the quake's rolling diminished to a shiver and then stopped.

Ross met Eveleen's eyes. She glanced toward the city, and he knew what she was thinking: their first task lay there, in those narrow streets, under stone buildings.

Linnea Edel had turned her eyes upward toward the portion of the volcano visible here. She licked her lips, then said, "I guess I'd better get busy looking for signs of nasty bald bad guys. The first order of business would be the local gossip center: AKA the oracle." She spoke in English, but no one corrected her.

Ashe only extended a hand, and the two started toward the steep trail zigzagging up the great mountain around the back of the city.

Ross extended a hand, using the same gesture, and Eveleen smiled at his irony. She unpacked one of the sample bolts of the linen that would be her entry to talk to people in the market.

Together they started up the shore toward the city, to begin investigating there. As he walked, Ross wondered who was the greater enemy, the Baldies or Nature.

Chapter Six

As always, the Time Agents were to interact on a personal level as little as possible. Gordon Ashe had kept himself alive by learning to blend in, and to keep his own counsel. His partners, on most runs, had been men; in most parts of the world during prehistory, women had not had the freedom of movement that the Time Agents required.

Of course there were female agents as well, and they'd been successfully deployed in places where they were needed. All those women, like Eveleen, had gone through training, and they, too, had learned to blend in, and to keep their own counsel.

So he watched, uncomfortable, when Linnea held out a hand to stop an older woman. She gestured, then said the ancient Hittite word that Jonathan's team had decided meant "oracle."

The older woman shook her head, looking puzzled. So Linnea repeated the word, only in Ancient Greek.

The woman's face cleared, and she let out a voluble stream, her hands swooping up the path behind her and gesturing to indicate what Ashe thought meant a cave.

"Please! More slow," Linnea said.

"We have only the one oracle who speaks to us from the Earth Goddess, through the Priestesses of the Serpent," the woman replied, enunciating very clearly and slowly. "Where are you from?"

"I come with traders, from Kemt." She gave the correct form for "the Black Land," the Nile Valley, which Egyptians differentiated from "the Red Land," the desert.

"Ah! Well, then. That explains it." The woman adjusted her robe, and wiped her forehead. "I have heard that you have many great oracles over the sea. Well, but here we have the one, and even the islanders come to our mountain to consult." She pointed up the steep cliffs behind Akrotiri.

"Has the oracle told people to go away from the island?" Linnea asked in a careful voice.

"Our goddess foretold the battle of the Great Snakes the season my daughter bore her first son, and many have gone to the far islands, including my daughter." The woman opened her hands, an age-old gesture of acceptance. "Me? It is my home here, for too many seasons to change, just because the earth spirits cannot rest, and the snake clouds form. They are distant, not here in our city."

"Many thanks, and blessings." Linnea's language was correct, but her body language was self-conscious, unnatural, as if she were very much aware of playing a part—as if she felt silly.

Ashe was relieved when the woman smiled sympathetically, repeated in a slow voice her directions, and added a wish for blessings in a soft voice. Sympathy, not suspicion.

His relief was short-lived.

They started at once up the path. Linnea seemed to relax now that they were alone. So did Ashe, but when his old and admired friend looked around and smiled and made exclamations from time to time in English, at first Ashe did not know what to do.

They began trudging up the sharply angled path that zig-zagged up the side of the great mountain. Their going was slow, partly because it would not do to go jogging straight up the mountain in what was going to be a very hot, humid day, partly because just ahead of them on the trail was a woman leading a laden donkey, and also because Linnea kept stopping in order to gaze at the half-ruined city of Akrotiri, which spread grandly along the base of the mountain.

"Oh, to explore every building!" she murmured softly.

Ashe did not answer. He kept moving.

Linnea turned her head, saw him a ways along the trail, and bustled to catch up.

Again they walked in silence, Ashe from time to time glancing up the mountain. From this angle he could see at least one great vent, from which smoke rose in lazy curls to join the thick haze higher up. He was not sure if there were others within his view, or if what seemed to be smoke was just air currents moving what had already risen.

"Oh! Here comes someone," Linnea whispered—again in English.

Ashe said nothing. He increased his pace slightly, to narrow the gap between them and the woman with the donkey.

An older man escorting two young girls came round the trail, the girls' earrings and skirts swinging. The younger one was chattering, apparently not noticing the looks of concern on the older girl's and the man's faces.

As they neared the woman on the donkey, they pressed into single file.

The woman looked up at the sky, as if noting the time, then said—in Ancient Greek—what sounded like, "You are today's first seeker, no? Did the goddess speak?"

"Not in a way I understand," the man said slowly, sighing. "And the priestesses only shake their heads and repeat what I was told by the goddess: that a shadow flies across the sun, and another shadow flies beyond that, silencing the earth spirits. She can hear nothing."

The younger girl looked up at the bright blue sky with a fearful glance and then they passed.

Ashe glanced once at Linnea. She had slipped behind him, her lips compressed, her eyes excited.

When the people were safely around the curve below, she murmured in a voice of delight, "Did you hear them? Just like that old lady. I understood! I comprehended! The accent we have learned for the Ancient Greek is not so very far off, no more than, say, BBC English is from a Texas accent." She smiled at Ashe, the old smile of discovery.

But mostly he was annoyed. So much so that he hesitated to speak.

Now the trail leveled out for a time, and even widened for what had to be a little rest stop under the shade of three scrabbled, pumice-dusted olive trees. Just behind them was a cracked basin, carved from the same lovely marblelike rock that most of the city was built of, with dolphins carved above it. They paused to look at it, saw the reddish marks of oxidation, realized it was there to catch runoff during the rainy season.

Ashe glanced down into the bottom of it, saw a wet layer of sediment mixed with the gray pebbly pumice they had seen everywhere else. It had rained, and fairly recently.

A shudder underfoot, and a low rumble, so low it was almost off the scale of human perception, startled them both. Tiny rocks came clattering down from above. One stung Ashe's cheek, and he saw Linnea bat at something and then turn her back.

The quake subsided, though the noise didn't. More people came down the trail, this time two older women.

And again the woman with the laden donkey said, "The goddess, did she speak to you?"

"Only of silence, a silence of shadows," one of the women said, and the other pursed her lips, looking out at the sea. "The same we have been hearing this three moons and past."

Twice more they encountered people coming down the trail, one of them riding a donkey, and with each the woman ahead asked her question, though with those she spoke a language that Ashe couldn't comprehend. But to her questions the people responded with headshakes and shrugs, age-old gestures.

Finally, just after the last one had vanished on the trail below, Linnea said—in English—"The 'oracle' seems to have nothing to say."

And Ashe said, in Ancient Greek, emulating the accent they had been hearing, "I do not understand you."

Linnea looked up with a brief smile that faded when she saw his expression. Her eyes narrowed, her expression now reflective.

She looked down at her sandals winking in and out below the hem of her bravely colored garment, and at last she said, in Greek this time, "I was wrong. It is not real to me."

To which Ashe replied, "It must become real. There is no record of a woman speaking a foreign tongue, surprising people with things that never have been."

Linnea's cheeks reddened. Again she ducked her head, and Ashe's irritation vanished. It wasn't as if she were the first to think of their guises as mere playacting.

Linnea Edel was a superb archaeologist whose specialty was volcanic sites. She'd been cramming, during their own training period, with all the new technology used by vulcanists.

She said, in a low voice, "I did not think about being a woman of the time, only seeing others of the time." A pause, and then, "I envisioned myself invisible to the people now, but I am not, am I?"

Ashe said, "You will be invisible, that is, leave no memory, if you behave as they expect."

Linnea nodded once.

Up ahead, the woman with the donkey said to a family starting down the trail, "Did the goddess speak to you?"

"No," said the family, even the children. The wife added, with a sour glance back, "We even offered our very best fish, fresh caught. But all she spoke of was silence and shadows. She did not forewarn us of the rock rain three moons ago." And, with a sidelong glance at her husband, she said, "I think the goddess has gone away, with the snake fires. I think we ought to hire a boat and go south with my family."

The husband did not respond, and the family moved on down the trail.

Ashe and Linnea kept walking. Not long after, they arrived at the top of a long shelf. A whisper of breeze came off the sea, cooling to their damp faces, but not quite diminishing the whiff of sulfur.

A small number of people stood before a great crack in the rock above the cliff, from which floated the faint sounds of young girls' voices rising and falling in a chant.

Striations of multicolored stone outlined the cave, whose mouth was dark. At the apex of this triangular cave faint wisps of vapor puffed out, swiftly dispersing; inside the cave somewhere had to be a hot stream.

That explained why the unseen oracle, or at least the oracle's attendants, had chosen that place. Water year-round in this climate, hot for cold days, plentiful (if slightly sulfuric) for the long rainless summers, would be important.

Ashe and Linnea edged round the back of the crowd waiting patiently. The woman with the donkey was, for the moment, the only one besides them moving. She plodded straight into the cave as one who had the right.

For a moment Ashe glimpsed robes dyed a robin's egg blue: a priestess. Then the woman had vanished inside, with the first of the waiting people.

Ashe stood in the lee of a great piece of sun-bleached pumice, probably from a blast a million years before, and glanced around. Ah. The smoke came from over there.

He touched Linnea's arm, and tipped his chin.

Her glance of longing was unmistakable, but she turned with no apparent resentment. Ashe felt a surge of relief, even gratitude. He had not wanted to admonish her; the risk was that the assumption of superiority would somehow cross professional lines into the personal. And maybe with a very young agent, it would have. They tended to take things personally, even if it was inadvertent.

Linnea just cast back one last glance of yearning. The archaeologist in her was intensely curious about the living ritual concerning an oracle. But now was not the time to witness it.

They edged along a narrow goat trail and began climbing up along the mountainside, away from the cliffside cave. They were very quickly out of sight of anyone below.

Up and up. The smell of sulfur got considerably stronger. Ashe stopped, holding his breath. Linnea, who had climbed behind him, winced, and mimed putting their breathing masks on.

It was a question. Ashe looked about and saw no one. He nodded, taking out his mask, and said in English, "There is nothing up here but rock and volcanic ash. I think the hydrogen sulfide would drive even the hardiest away—and the locals must know by now how swiftly death can come from these vents."

Linnea nodded, passed a hand inside her robes, and pulled out the cloth-disguised breather that the scientific team had fashioned for her.

Ashe had on his own. The air smelled of plastic, and slightly stale, but the mask successfully absorbed the potentially deadly gases. A small strip of chemplast, visible from the corner of his vision, would change color if the concentration became too much for the mask to handle; another indicated the mask's remaining capacity. Both were green.

They climbed on, easing around a crumbling rock, and felt intense heat. The hardy little tufts of grass and weed that they had seen here and there, more evidence that the rainy season had begun, had long since withered away.

Another ten paces and air shimmered from escaping heat. Ashe paused to glance out toward the sea. Tiny boats and single-masted ships dotted the horizon.

"Go ahead," he said. "I'll do a visual scan."

Linnea nodded once, her intense investigative expression widening her eyes again, She opened her robe, revealing plain cotton shorts and a fine cotton-silk undershirt beneath. Round her waist she wore a sturdy belt, onto which, like a superhero of the comic books, she'd attached pouches and holders.

She unclipped several vulcanology instruments—infrared thermosensor, a sensitive sniffer to measure gas types and concentrations, and other devices Ashe didn't recognize—then edged closer to the vent in order to start recording.

Ashe turned in the other direction, pulled out the mini—field glasses the science team had furnished him, and shaded them with one hand so the glass wouldn't glint in the sun as he closely and minutely swept the bay.

Bravely decorated boats circled about, some hung with decorations from prow to stern, others painted along the sides with leaping dolphins and swarming octopi, some with stylized lilies and crocuses. The people, flattened by the distance, talked back and forth or rowed, or sailed, or fished, or gazed off into the distance. These, then, were the people the scientists called "the squatters"—the people who remained behind after the first great quake that destroyed parts of the city and who had begun to rebuild.

What exactly was he seeking? Some anomaly, some sign that there were others here, perhaps in disguise as well, from the future.

A sigh made him turn around. Linnea was holding one of the instruments he hadn't recognized, a flattened ovoid with a pistol grip. He saw the tendons in her hand flex as she pulled the trigger: a click, a whirr, and several sets of antennae uncurled from the front and fanned out rigidly. She stared down at the instruments and then pulled the trigger again, and the antennae curled back into the casing.

Linnea crossed to his side. "Well, the brains at home will love these readings," she said. "Isotope concentrations and types, gas readings, just about everything is either off the scale or close as makes no difference." She hefted the odd instrument. "The piezo-EM strain detector, too—and it's not terribly sensitive."

"Meaning?" Ashe asked, though he knew.

"Even without strain readings from fixed laser interferometers, which we didn't bring because we don't have time for them, everything points to a big blow, bigger than anything recorded in modern times. Far bigger," she added seriously.

So it was time for Ashe's own test.

He unclipped from his belt a flat meter that was about the size of a video cam. Inside it, though, was a little of the strange tech that had come from the future by way of the past, about which they were still learning. The materials, how they produced their strange effects, including their signature temporal distortion, were still largely a mystery, but scientists, patiently experimenting for twenty-five years, had learned to use the tech for several applications useful to Project Star.

He tabbed the power on and watched the little LED screen light up. Then it was his turn to brave the ferocious heat of the vent, as close as he could get, holding out his meter.

The graph bar on it trembled but did not move.

They looked at each other. Despite the danger, he'd have to get closer.

Ashe edged closer, hearing a whooshing rumble deep below, as if air were being forced through inconceivably big compressors.

Suddenly the graph bar flickered and then leaped halfway across the little screen.

Ashe moved the meter in a slow half circle, just to make certain. The graph bar held... held... diminished down to nothing when he moved it away from the vent.

Back again. And again, it snapped into a long rectangle, which meant only one thing.

He edged back down to where Linnea waited. He did not know what his face showed, but she seemed to read something there, for she said, "You found it?"

He nodded once. "Somewhere in that vent is Baldy tech."

Chapter Seven

The entire western horizon was a deep crimson, the bottoms of the approaching march of sheep-backed clouds bluish, the tops the gold of fire. It was a spectacular sunset, almost garish and almost sinister in its intensity.

A volcanic sunset. But none of the six Time Agents noticed it; they were all staring in grim dismay at the destruction of their campsite. Destruction and disappearance: their tents, bedrolls, and the food that the Greek agents had unloaded were all gone. Everything else lay scattered about—broken open by violent hands, rifled through, and then discarded.

"Everything?" Ross asked finally, turning over a pottery fragment with his sandaled foot. He recognized that pot: it had held their oatmeal mix, carefully made to look like regular oats, but vitamin and protein fortified.

"Everything," Stavros said. "Except the last load from the ship." He jerked a thumb behind him at the cloth-wrapped burdens he and Kosta had set down when they discovered the ruined site. "Our gear." He said the words in a low voice, in English: their radio and recording equipment, which would never be left alone.

Ashe, Ross, and Eveleen spontaneously turned, looking outward for signs of incipient attack. Linnea Edel stood, hands cradling her elbows, looking apprehensive.

There was nothing to be seen except the smoke-pall over the sky, the greenish choppy sea, and the barren land stretching in folds toward the sudden, dramatic cliffs along which was built Akrotiri. Behind the warehouse, the desolate land stretched away, dotted with quake-cracked hills and falls of rock, as seabirds circled overhead.

"Baldies," Ross stated. "And one of them is probably lying up on one of those cliffs somewhere now, watching our reaction through a high-tech field glass and gloating. Damn."

"We can't know that," Ashe said. And, to Kosta, "What exactly happened? Did you see or speak with anyone?"

"No," Kosta said. "We chose this empty warehouse, cleared out recently from the looks of things, because it was the very last, the farthest from the city. No people around. Those over there—" he indicated one of the other warehouses, the closest about five hundred yards away, the others lying along the gentle hills in the direction of the city "—we kept them in sight most of the time. The people in that one were all busy with their fish. That was another reason we chose this location." He smiled grimly; when the sluggish air moved, it carried a strong smell of fish. "We did not think this place would be watched."

Ashe nodded. "Baldies might assume that time travelers might come here first and hide equipment. We probably ought to have foreseen that."

"With all our things disguised?" Eveleen asked.

No one answered. She looked around, then sighed. "Yes, we probably would have been on the watch here, too—if we expected unwanted visitors showing up from the past."

"We had just finished unloading the camp gear, and had started setting it up," Kosta said. "Then went back together so we could make the last trip in one session."

"Told you I should have stayed," Stavros muttered in Modern Greek, his big hands tight on the hilt of the knife he wore at his side, his brows a single furrowed line.

"We don't know how many any more than we know who," Ashe reminded everyone. "All right. Then we go immediately to our fallback plan: the men will sleep on the boat with the gear." He pointed to their disguised equipment. "Eveleen, you are in charge of finding us an observation base within the safety of the city."

Eveleen nodded.

"Then let's eat," Ashe said, "and get moving."

Shortly afterward they sat on a grassy crag overlooking Akrotiri, eating the barley-and-lentil flatbread that Eveleen had bought hot from the oven, crumbled goat cheese on the top, and for dessert fresh-picked grapes. Ross and Kosta had carried the precious gear back to the boat, where Kosta stayed on guard.

The setting was pretty, a green little shelter carved by runoff, the view spectacular, the food actually quite tasty, but no one was in a good mood.

"So they're here." Ross spoke finally, surprised he felt more satisfaction than any other emotion.

Of course. It was because the presence of the Baldies gave them a purpose, a direction, a goal. Something definite to aim for, accomplish—and then get out.

Stavros grinned, a brief, somewhat martial flash of teeth that was easy enough for Ross to interpret: Stav, and Kosta as well, welcomed more than feared the prospect of the Baldies trying to find and get aboard their ship.

Ashe, noting Stav's reaction, did not hide his snort of amusement. He said, "Just as well you'll be working off some of that hotheadedness with me up on the mountain."

Stavros and Ross both grinned. Ashe gave Ross a wry look, then turned back to Stavros. "And you can begin working it off by getting the gear up there."

Stavros laughed. "With all respect, I shall permit a donkey to bear it instead."

"And you get to coax the donkey. My guess is that'll be work enough," Ashe retorted.

Stavros opened his palm. "Ah, it is true enough. Even 3,600 years up-time, the beasts have wicked tempers. I do not expect them to be sweeter now."

"So would I if my existence was defined as 'beast of burden,' " Eveleen put in. "Well, I'm ready to go."

Ashe said, "Let's get back to the ship and get a good night's rest. Tomorrow will be rough."

Tomorrow's roughness began shortly after midnight, when blue lightning ripped through the stifling heat. With the first crack of thunder came hail. It drummed on the canopy, which was made of treated cloth indistinguishable from contemporary material—except that it was quite waterproof. Stavros, on current watch, could just be heard swearing as he hastily got under cover.

As abruptly as it had started, the hail turned into rain, a gritty, eye-stinging rain full of volcanic ash. Despite the canopy's shelter the normal working of the boat let the water seep in, and some dripped down onto Ross's face. In the reflected blue glare of more lightning he saw the others in their hammocks, eyes open, faces bespattered with dirty, stinging drips of rain.

No one spoke. At least the hail and rain flattened the sea down substantially; the boat had been rocking fretfully since they'd retired.

The rain continued, a dull, steady roar, and Ross closed his eyes again. He was on the edge of chill; he reached for the fake fur rolled up on a tiny shelf above his hammock, cast it over himself, and as warmth returned, so did drowsiness. Despite the fury of the storm, he was soon asleep.

When they woke up, the air was washed clean, the breeze from the west pure and brisk.

Konstantin had prepared breakfast for them before coming below to retire. Fresh-caught fish, grilled over an open fire, and more of the flatbread constituted the meal. Smelling it, Eveleen felt her mouth water. Her head felt clear, and she smiled at the clean blue sky in the west.

A glance eastward, though, diminished her good mood. There was the ubiquitous smoke, slowly drifting westward as the breeze died. The volcanic smog was making a comeback.

As Eveleen ate in silence, she listened to Ross and Ashe talk in low voices with Stavros, planning how they would get the heat resistant suits up the mountain without calling attention to themselves. The proof that the Baldies were definitely here had caused the first rule to be implemented: their cautionary radio silence was now, except for dire emergency, total.

The Baldies were here.

Linnea voiced a worry when the women waded ashore and started up the trail toward the city. "Do you think that attack on our camp was the Baldies, then? If so, why?"

Eveleen gave her head a shake. Of course Linnea had been fully briefed on what little they knew of the Baldies. It was so little, missing any hint of motivation, that Eveleen knew that personal experience would be more convincing than mere reference to old reports. "I can't guess. So far, the Baldies have not exactly been subtle when they see us. If that was them, it could have been a test, or a warning, even. They obviously didn't want to risk being seen, for they could easily have waited and attacked Stav and Kosta. Seen or heard: the men would have set up a shout, and maybe those fishers would have come running. The camp attack was probably done fast and silent."

Linnea nodded and blanched slightly. Eveleen wondered if she was thinking of the Baldies' efforts in human mind control, which had worked with unpredictable results. Ross's scarred hand was one result, though admittedly he had been wearing one of their shimmery-fabric suits when it occurred. "I don't think the Baldies could do their mind tricks with a whole crowd of determined fishers. I think they have to concentrate on us one at a time. And as for the ship being attacked next, Stav and Kosta have it well protected. They won't get it as easily as they got that camp."

"All right, then," Linnea said, in a determinedly bright voice. "So let's see if we can find anything that might answer some of our questions." She smiled. "And at the same time regard this as a shopping opportunity of a lifetime."

Eveleen laughed. When they reached the spot where the trail joined a bigger road, packed hard from years of pounding by biped and quadruped feet, they fell silent, melding into the crowd heading toward Akrotiri.

The clatter of voices rose around them. Eveleen listened to everyday chatter as they neared the great gates. The sacred horns rose against the sky, silhouetted against the milky blue. Already the volcanic haze was spoiling the pure brilliance of morning.

Linnea clutched her basket protectively against her. It was an ordinary basket heaped with small packages wrapped in cloth and leather. The ones on top were indeed the food they were meant to suggest; her equipment nestled underneath. Eveleen preferred wearing hers under her clothing, to keep her hands free.

Not that there was any overt threat here. Eveleen realized that Linnea had stopped, and alarm flared briefly through her until she saw Linnea resting her basket on a low wall as she watched a group of magnificently dressed young women parading down the street, their arms full of crocus flowers. Somehow, somewhere, someone had managed to grow flowers, despite the increasingly cruel slaps of Nature all around them.

Eveleen, staring after them, remembered how often she'd read statements about human adaptability. Here was living proof. She realized she'd expected furtive sneaking about, or outright fear, and not people laughing, talking, carrying on with their lives.

A group of younger girls, sudden as starlings, danced around them, singing, their voices high and birdlike in the open air.

Linnea drew a deep breath.

"The saffron makers," Eveleen guessed, remembering her research.

A single nod.

The procession wound its way past them, making for one of the great buildings in which religious ceremonies took place. As they wound their way along the narrow street, they could still hear singing coming from the open windows of a low building that was still left standing.

Pungent smells assailed them: fish, goat, the pervasive stink of burning rock. Dyers stirred great pots, the fires beneath pale in the glary light. Strong herbal odors drifted on the thick, dusty air. At the sides of the street rubble had been piled neatly; men of various ages swarmed about the bigger piles, some putting down big jagged pieces of stone, others taking them to carts and hauling them away—instant recycling.

Eveleen realized that Linnea had become so mesmerized watching the cloth makers, the potters, the seed grinders and bakers, she'd forgotten about their orders to watch for signs of Baldies' presence before the bedazzlement of seeing living, breathing people performing the homey, everyday activities that scholars far on the other side of the mists of time would spend hours speculating about.

Eveleen didn't remind her. Experience had taught her that this sort of academic reverie was actually trustworthy: an expert would see an anomaly at least as fast as, maybe even faster than, the more mission-focused observer. It was just very slow going. After a time, Eveleen got tired of watching bartering and looked around for signs of rebuilding. She wondered why Linnea seemed so intent on these little exchanges of goods for goods, until she finally realized that what Linnea was looking for was evidence of someone writing.

A flare of humor almost caused Eveleen to laugh. Linnea Edel was an unreconstructed academic, even after their hasty training: she was not looking for Baldies; she was on the lookout for someone carving Linear A hieroglyphs into clay, so that she could confirm or refute recent scholarship on its decoding!

Ought she to say something? No. Her instinct was good. If Linnea was watching people that closely, she might notice something Eveleen wouldn't.

On they walked, back and forth up the hill, along narrow streets with hot sun reflecting heat waves in almost visible sheets. Twice minor tremors caused people to halt, to shift their eyes anxiously up, or down, to pause in conversation, but when the earthquake died, work and talk resumed, in several languages.

"...I heard the goddess has still not spoken," an old woman told another in Ancient Greek, as they portioned out water in tiny red-clay cups from a great urn.

"Not for three moons. It is why my sister and her family decided to sail. I believe we must wait and be patient. She has always spoken to us before."

"True, true. She will speak when speech becomes necessary. So I tell my son, who fears for the children. He says times have become so strange, with both fire and water rising from the earth, and rocks falling from the sky, he fears the goddess has departed, leaving us to the fire spirits."

A long sigh was the answer, and the two women turned away.

Eveleen and Linnea walked on, Eveleen watching the movements of the people. Un-self-conscious, busy, socializing as they worked, they all appeared to be genuine Kallistans. Eveleen knew that she must look for anything out of place, but she kept envisioning Baldies shrouded in cloth, lurking about on the edges of crowds. Watching for them? Surely they would not interact with the people any more than she and Linnea must, except in the most superficial manner. *We must not stand out*, Eveleen thought. *We are aliens to the Baldies, which is a kind of protection if we are careful not to make any mistakes. If they are searching for us, we must remain indistinguishable from all these others.*

"Grapes?" A gentle hand nudged her arm. "Grapes? Grown well away from the smoke, tasting sweet?"

A young girl looked up into Eveleen's face, gold earrings very much like her own swinging next to dusky-colored-cheeks. Candid brown eyes assessed her, and then the girl repeated her question in two other tongues.

Eveleen wet her lips, and then said in Ancient Greek, "I have been thinking about grapes."

The dark brows arched in surprise. "Ah! You will find that mine are sweetest. Here. Taste one." Nimble fingers twisted at a plump grape at the top of the basket.

Eveleen smiled as she glimpsed the older, slightly withered ones beneath. *The girl's sales wiles would probably work better on those young men over there, building the ship*, she thought. But she tasted the grape, which had the same slightly bitter tang as those she'd bought the day before.

"Eh," she said.

The girl's face altered into intent: now it was time to bargain.

As they embarked on their exchange, Eveleen was peripherally aware of Linnea looking in one direction, a slight frown between her brows.

She finished her bargain more hastily than she'd intended, and held out her hand. The girl glanced down at the little bits of lapis lazuli the scientists three thousand years into the future had furnished for everyday trade, scrupulously took two of the smallest, and stashed them in her skirt.

Then with a cheery wave she was gone, and a moment later Eveleen was vaguely aware of her sweet voice again, "Grapes! Sweet grapes?"

Eveleen dropped the bright blue bits of lapis into the pocket in her skirt, aware of Linnea sighing with regret as she watched the young woman walk away.

"What is it?" she murmured in Ancient Greek.

"If I could just hear repeated, slowly, her words in all those tongues, I could find Ancient Greek cognates in whatever it is these people talk among themselves when traders from the other Cyclades Islands are not around."

Linear A again, *Eveleen thought with a spurt of amusement.* Detectives on a murder case have nothing on archaeologists for single-mindedness!

But then she realized Linnea was frowning back in the other direction. "What is it?" she murmured, looking at some brightly woven rugs hanging over a dusty stone wall that ended abruptly just above a landslide.

"Is there something odd about that little square over there?" Linnea asked, her chin lifting slightly off to the right.

Eveleen helped herself to one of the grapes she'd stashed in a shawl sling she'd fashioned from extra fabric, and as she chewed she glanced casually up, sweeping the right.

Nothing looked out of place. In booths marked by low stone walls, built round a tiny side square with mats fixed up as temporary shelter, a man was busy beating bronze sheets into tools; several cheerfully naked small children played a game with smooth pebbles; an old, toothless woman expertly spun thread through her fingers. On the other side, several young girls were busy winnowing fava seeds from beans, singing quietly and without much joy.

Distracted, Eveleen watched the girls tossing aside black-spotted, withered beans, their gestures expressive of reluctance, of worry: clearly a poor harvest. The older women watched, one singing. Another was getting the shelled seeds ready for sun drying, her lips pressed together in a tight line. Others ground dried beans with round stone mills, their song soft and soothing.

What else was there to notice? Eveleen looked more closely at the people as she and Linnea moved slowly along. Linnea stooped to examine bronze tools being made, then straightened up, shaking her head. The artisan, seeing her, turned his shoulder, and Linnea breathed, "House. Next to the monkeys."

Eveleen did another casual sweep, this time scanning behind the people and along the buildings. The primary building near them was a house with three low windows and one door around which were painted dancing monkeys in a graceful pattern. Above each window there was a long-tailed swallow painted, bright blue, each bird flying upward.

The front of the house looked intact, but one could see through the gaping windows that the roof had fallen in, and no one was inside.

Those swallows definitely caught the eye, Eveleen thought, glancing at the women going in and out of a smaller jury-rigged building adjacent. Next to that was a smaller house, somewhat tucked back, very plain—like so many along the streets. No one went in, no one came out, and there was no one visible in the one window.

Linnea walked on and examined fabric draped over a low window adjacent to the two houses. Eveleen bent over the rough cloth, brightly dyed blue and red in lovely patterns that would appeal to people in modern times, but she forced herself to observe beyond the heads of the spinners sitting inside the window. Now she was looking across the little court.

Then she saw it: people walked in and out of all the few whole buildings along the street, in and out of shacks, lean-tos, tents draped from old walls, and mat-covered awnings—every structure, in short, except that one.

As she watched, one of the pebbles from the children's game bounced in the direction of the mystery house. A child ran to get it, his steps faltered, though there was no apparent barrier, then he reached down and snatched up his stone and retreated in haste.

"Force field?" Eveleen whispered. And, with an inward pang, "I should have seen that."

Linnea turned away from the fabric and murmured as she rummaged in her basket, "You were watching the people, as is right. But we archaeologists...we are trained to observe the negative spaces, you might say."

Such as no one going in and out of a specific building—something Eveleen had not considered.

"What now?" Linnea asked, bending to look at urns full of dried lentils, all dusted with ash.

"Mark the place, report to the others. Keep looking."

"How do we mark it?" Linnea asked.

Eveleen fingered a rug. "Make a mental map. I'll do that."

They kept moving, Eveleen itching to get back and investigate that mysterious little house. But she forced herself to keep moving along the narrow little streets, though now her observations were at best perfunctory.

Nothing. Nothing. No sign of Baldies...no signs at all.

At the very top, they stood in a faint breeze and looked down at the jumble of ruins, hide and reed-mat roofs, and rubble piles below them. "All right, now we try it, just to see how far we get, and what happens," Eveleen whispered.

Linnea nodded once, swallowing visibly.

They bought more cheese on the way down, and fresh bread, all piled into Linnea's basket. Eveleen led the way to their little court. The children were all eating now, except for two of them asleep on rugs next to walls that cast a bit of shade. The women with the fava beans still worked. The spinner leaned out a window, talking in a low voice to a man who held a donkey by a rope, the animal still except for the switching of its tail to chase flies away.

No one was near the plain building.

Eveleen rummaged at her pouch, closed her hands round lapis rocks, pretended to stumble, and cast the blue stones that way. Only one rolled in the right direction. She gave a cry of dismay and chased after them, Linnea with her.

One, two, three, and there was the fourth, over by that empty door. She started over and faltered when danger prickled down the back of her neck, tightening her shoulder blades. She glanced behind her: no one there. No one paid her the least attention.

A step, another, and her fingers closed around the stone.

It wasn't a force field, then; it was some kind of mental impulse or even just subsonics. She permitted herself one glance inside that open door.

Nothing.

She turned away, put her lapis lazuli into her pouch, and fought the instinct to look back.

"All right, we know there's something weird there," she murmured.

Linnea nodded once. "And now we have to find a market spot or at least an apartment. Do you want to negotiate or shall I?"

Her tone of voice, so polite, indicated she wanted to try. From what Eveleen had seen, the older women commanded the most authority, if not respect. So she shook her head. "You do it. I want to watch some more."

They continued on, Linnea now seeking the best vantage. Eveleen's mind was back on that strange room.

The place Linnea chose was next to the building that evidently belonged to the Priestesses of the Serpent, which showed the most signs of repair of any. Not just young women about to embark on religious duties stayed there, but it seemed to be a kind of hotel, or hostel, for women from the harbor. Linnea successfully negotiated a little room, and no one gave them any false reaction, any strange questions, any sign of trouble. Eveleen stood at the one window and looked down at the sweep of market and the edge of the harbor. It was a prime spot for observation.

Yet her shoulder blades stayed tight all the rest of the day.

Chapter Eight

"It wasn't there. At least, that's what our instruments tell us now."

Silence.

Ross braced himself for the stupid questions. They didn't come. Linnea Edel, who had been with Ashe when they had discovered the alien tech in the vent, looked surprised, but then she sat back, folded her hands, and waited.

"So we tested again, with Ross's equipment, and it came up as negative as mine."

Silence again. Eveleen rubbed her thumbnail along her bottom lip, then said, "So, what, they have detectors on their device that registers pings?"

"It would appear so," Ashe said.

"Then they definitely know we're here," Linnea murmured, looking about in question.

"That makes it more convincing that it was a Baldy welcome committee that tossed our camp," Ross stated.

They sat in the boat, under cover of truly inky darkness. Thick clouds, mixed with smoke, obscured the sky. The water was fretful, with little shivering rows of choppy waves—the result of several minor quakes all through the evening. There was a sharp smell in the air, a combination of hot rock, ozone, and sulfur that mixed unpleasantly with brine.

Ashe finally stretched out his feet tiredly and said, "Yet we still haven't seen them. Well, to the rest of our report. We put on the flame suits and our breathing masks and went down as far as we could, doing infrared scans as well as Baldy-tech pings, but of course we had no idea what to expect. We didn't know if it had been moved, turned off, or cloaked; whether or not it would be buried or in plain sight; how big it would be." He sat back and reached for one of the disguised flagons of pure water.

Ross said, "What 'looking around' really means is we slipped and sweated in the darkness until it was too damn hot to do anything but broil. The coolers on those suits don't have enough capacity for really long searches; they need a lot more. I wish we could score a few of the Baldy suits."

Their suits used the same technique as space suits: tubes running throughout the thick insulated fabric carried cooling fluid all over the body. He recalled that shimmering blue-green fabric that the Baldies used not just as clothing but also as insulation, filters, and conduits for their mysterious mental radar. Its insulation function actually included refrigeration, preventing heat from entering while exhausting heat from the interior as needed, operating on the same strange power source as all the Baldy tech. Which was why they couldn't bring the stuff they'd captured: the Baldies would have known they were there the moment they pushed through the time-gate.

Ashe said, "So what did you women find, besides a base for observation?"

Linnea opened her hand in a little gesture toward Eveleen, who said, "A house, seems to be empty, with some kind of mental repulsion field or subsonics. No other sign."

Ross frowned. "Could be a trap. To see who pokes around."

Eveleen nodded once. "I thought of that while we were waiting for you. In any case, we only checked it once, and didn't go back."

Ashe said, "Why don't we investigate the buildings around it, then, and see what we find?" He nodded at Linnea. "Eveleen can take one of the suits and my gear and help Ross up on the mountain."

Ross knew what that meant: a long, dreary day of trudging up, searching for vents, and checking them, in case the mysterious device had been put into another vent. Having Eveleen come along was his way of acknowledging a spectacularly dangerous and tiring day's work.

"Oh, thanks," Eveleen said, and the others chuckled. She turned Linnea's way. "At least one of us will get a thrill, eh?"

"Oh, it seems to me that there might be potential thrills enough in exploring volcanic vents," Linnea said, smiling. "But I confess: to see the spectacular frescoes inside those buildings still standing when the paintings are still relatively fresh and new, and not crumbled and age-ruined, would be a joy I'd never forget."

Ashe nodded and then turned to Stavros. "Any suspicious activity to report on the waterfront?"

"No sign of Baldies—no attempted attacks, overt or covert. The fishermen are upset about the numbers of dead fish," Stavros said. "The water temperature is several degrees higher than it ought to be, which would be devastating for many types of fish. It's apparently worse closer to the pre-Kameni Island."

The pre-Kameni Island did not even exist up the time-line. Ross mentally examined the map of the island complex: Kalliste and its appendages looked, to him, like nothing so much as a blob of dough floating in the middle of a donut with a bite out of it. The mountain up behind them was, of course, only a small part of the biggest, crescent-shaped island on which they now stood. The caldera would be about eighty miles in diameter; its center—the dough blob—was, according to the scientists' models, the island that Ross could see lying north of them. This little island, which would be blasted into nothingness during the Big Blow, had been termed *pre-Kameni* by the scientists.

Ross remembered watching it earlier, through field glasses, from one of the western cliffs. They could just make out buildings there, most of them ruins, with some little boats plying round it. Squatters there, too, but very few of them.

Kosta said, in his heavy accent, "The people are worried that the oracle does not speak. The harvest is worse than anyone remembers, the quakes worse, the biggest one three months ago sending up serpents of fire-spewing smoke and bringing down a rain of pumice. Abruptly the quakes have eased since then, but the smoke is worse. Fish dead. They are afraid the gods are angry and won't talk to them through their oracle anymore."

Ashe looked over at Linnea. "Can we become a new oracle, as a last resort, to save lives? There are far too many people here. I do not want to see them incinerated without at least trying to get them to flee."

She shook her head. "You cannot just 'be' a new oracle, not here where there is only one, and that one sanctioned by the local governing body. Perhaps we could come down the mountain wailing about the oracle speaking at last and trust to the grapevine to spread the news."

"Will they listen?" Ross asked, skeptical.

Linnea's considering gaze turned his way. "They have no reason not to believe. The question involves community, though. People might want to question more closely who we are."

"That's right," Ashe said. "We are known as Egyptian traders, but we still are not identified with any kinship group. I don't know if that will suffice to get them to evacuate their homes."

Ross said with grim humor, "Right. There is no Red Cross waiting to help them, no friendly government wanting to aid refugees."

Ashe turned back to Linnea. "You or Eveleen might have to try to get inside the oracle caves, if the priestesses will talk to you."

"Better than the alternative," Ross muttered, but under his breath.

"Let's keep that as a backup plan, then," Ashe said, and no one disagreed.

They finished eating dinner, and as everyone was tired, their heads slightly aching from the oppressive heat and the polluted air, the men camped out on the deck of the ship under the stars, and Eveleen and Linnea used oil-soaked torches to light their way back to their rented room, Eveleen sleeping near the open window, where the slightest sound would waken her instantly.

Just before dawn the women hiked back down to the boat.

"The way I see it," Ross said to Eveleen a couple hours later, as they trudged up the long switchback trail toward the oracle, "is that it was too easy. A vent right around the corner from the oracle? We should have seen that as a setup."

Eveleen said, "What I'm afraid of is that they have put some kind of thingie in a whole slew of vents. What the heck do we do then?"

"Gordon said the same thing when we were thumping our way back down the mountain yesterday, nearly quaking off the trail once or twice."

"Then he thinks it probable." Eveleen heaved a sharp sigh and paused at a turning in the trail. She looked out at the blue-green ocean, deceptively placid in the hazy early morning light. "Vents. Does that mean—"

"Already thought of it," Ross said, grinning. "While you were in the sweatbox, Gordon told Stav to do some diving and exploring. The boys are taking the boat out to pre-Kameni Island today to do just that."

Sweatbox: their unfond name for the tiny shower cubicle the scientists had built into the stern of the boat. Ross thought of that cramped space—the banged elbows and knees as he tried to manipulate the spray hose and the lukewarm water—and laid himself a hundred-buck bet none of the science jockeys back home actually had test-driven the blasted thing.

"Here's the goat trail we marked yesterday," Ross said. "We may's well start here."

The two of them checked the pathway in both directions and then quickly eased off down the narrow little trail. There was very little brush behind which to hide. They would have to trust to the haze and to their neutral clothing—Eveleen had forgone her bright kilt-skirt and jacket-underdress for a plain robe of dusty brown—to avoid notice.

Ross squinted against the fierce glare of the sun, looking for the thin thread of smoke he'd seen wisping out of the mountain in this direction. These things could be deceptive, depending on air currents and wind.

Up, up, pausing for sips of water in the sparse shade of smoke-withered olive trees. Eveleen bent once to touch one of the lovely red lilies. Ross grimaced, thinking of the report he'd seen three thousand years up-time: these plants were totally wiped out. Some life-forms came back. The red lilies didn't.

They came upon the vent suddenly, feeling it first as an oven blast of sulfuric air.

After consultation with Ashe and Linnea over breakfast, they had agreed no longer to use the Baldy-tech device. They would scan with their own equipment, which used only pulses of sonic energy and heavy-duty computing power to filter out the returns from seismic noise. There was a lot of that on Kalliste, unfortunately, the upside being that their little pings were unlikely to be detected by the Baldies amidst the stew of heat, sonics, and piezo-EM emitted by the volcano.

Ross held his breath against the hot gases, knowing he should slip on his breathing mask. But the tests ought to take only a moment, and it didn't smell as bad as it had the other day. Then he remembered the basic vulcanology training all the agents had gotten: *By the time you stop smelling it, it's already too late. Hydrogen sulfide is fifty times more poisonous than hydrogen cyanide, and far more insidious. It just takes one sudden puff from a vent.*

He put on his mask and motioned Eveleen to do the same. Theoretically, if there was another of those devices, the sonics would reveal it, and since it had to be manipulating the ferocious energy output of the vents in some way, the strains and currents that it produced in rocks and lava would help disclose its shape.

They each took a reading, looked, but were not really sure what they had. There were patterns, but nothing suggested an actual object. Ross motioned to Eveleen and she held up her instrument to reveal the IR port. Ross triggered the link, and the two machines compared and manipulated the stored sonic patterns. Now a shadowy shape emerged, too regular to be natural. But the devices still couldn't nail down its distance or size well enough. "Well, now we know that they didn't move it."

"Why can't the detectors resolve it better?"

"Maybe there's too much seismic noise and it's turned off, or maybe it's still running cloaked but emitting sonics as part of its operation. That would scramble things. Let's find another and give the computers more to compare," Ross suggested. "Maybe then they can zero in on it."

"Right."

First to locate another vent.

"There." Eveleen knocked against his arm and pointed upward, almost straight into the sun, which was burning down through thick haze just behind the mountaintop.

"Oh, hell," Ross snarled.

"Yeah, looks like my idea of it, too," his wife retorted.

Ross cracked a smile, and they got busy toiling upward along tiny goat trails, often slipping and sliding in fresh rockfalls. They removed their masks once they were a good distance from the vent; it was a hot, exceedingly dangerous climb, made worse by the weather.

They stopped at noon to eat their bread and cheese and rest in the shade of a spectacular slab of volcanic rock thrusting up from some age-old eruption.

Out over the ocean a thin line of thunderheads marched, their outline ragged. The sea was a sick green, the sunny glare at its worst, glinting off bits of rock. Far below they could see a steady procession of folk making their way slowly up the pathway to the oracle.

"Why would people do that to themselves?" Ross said, shaking his head.

"Why do people in our day read weather reports, or even check the astrology predictions in the paper, much as they laugh?"

"Eveleen, it's too hot to even pretend that's the same as gambling their lives against whatever this 'oracle' might say."

"But I think it's the same impulse. We don't like going into the unknown. So we use whatever tools we have. The weather reports generally work. The astrology predictions speak so generally you can always translate them to match your experience. And these people—" She waved her hand up the trail. "Well, who knows? Linnea told me that one theory holds that the priestesses who served the oracle had the best gossip network going and knew everything about everyone. I guess you could do that with a small population. Remember, even modern market research relies on something called the Delphi effect—you can get information out of large groups of people even if none of them know the actual, exact answer."

Ross raised an eyebrow, but Eveleen's face was serious. Well, there were a lot of things he'd never heard of; evidently the Delphi effect was one of them. He sighed. "It makes sense if people are asking whether or not they should marry some person with a rotten rep, or even about crops and other information based on collective experience and knowledge, but what about this couple we saw yesterday, with a sick kid? They wanted to know if the wasting fever would go away."

Eveleen rested her hands on her knees. "Of course they couldn't really answer something like that, but they probably told the people to make a flower offering to the gods, which at least would give them comfort."

"Some comfort."

"About as much comfort as We shall have to do more tests,' gives parents in our time, when their kid has some disease the medical field can't identify."

Ross wiped sweat off his forehead. "Hah."

Eveleen grinned. "You're just grumpy because it's hot, and there's thunder in the air, and no enemy to shoot at."

"Add in a mountain-size nuclear bomb under our feet or, knowing the Baldies, something even worse, ready to blow at any moment, and you've got that right."

Somehow that seemed the right moment to get to their feet, stash their flagons at their waists, and get moving.

The climb was long, hot, and increasingly steep. Rock slides were common, making the ground unstable. Tiny tremors sent pebbles skittering down the mountain, bouncing crazily. They both were stung on hands and faces by tiny bits of rock.

They worked their way steadily upward, the trail carrying them northward over the spectacular cliffs and great, violent upthrusts of rock, until they were able to get glimpses of the northern segment of the crescent-shaped island, with the doomed little pre—Kameni Island hazily lying to the west. Smoke rose slowly from distant vents, adding to the brownish-gray pall.

Conversation became impossible. The thick air was made thicker by sulfurous stenches. They realized at about the same time that their increasingly intense headaches were not caused by the heat and slipped on their breathing masks, which indicated that they were being exposed to dangerous gases, hydrogen sulfide foremost among them. And though no one was around to see them, they still followed orders, both swathing their heads and lower faces with lengths of rough cloth to hide the masks.

Their headaches faded away slowly as the breathing masks removed the dangerous gases from the air. The relief gave them both energy, and they picked up their pace again. As they climbed toward what appeared to be the summit, the thunderheads sailed inexorably toward them, lightning occasionally flashing down to stab the sea.

They were high enough now to look directly down into the clear, blue-green water. Now they could see some of the underwater vents releasing vapors that heated the water within the ring: these were discolored silver-green in some places, and in one or two an ominous rusty-tinged green, like an old bruise. Above the sea hung strange palls of dust and smoke tinged with a sinister orange.

Ross nodded, and Eveleen took out her palm-sized video cam, sweeping the scene with care. "I wish I could see Akrotiri from here," she murmured.

"Maybe higher up," Ross said. "Though the distance will make it look like a toy city."

Eveleen nodded, tucking the cam securely into her belt-pouch. "Let's go."

They trudged up the last distance to what had to be a gigantic vent. Ross, ceaselessly watching for signs of Baldies standing guard, kept his hand near his side, where he wore a weapon. Memories of his hand burning, of helping Ashe cross-country with a bullet wound in his shoulder, made him wary.

At last they reached the vent.

Whose instinct reacted first?

Before he saw anything except swirling smoke and vapor, Ross knew there was someone in that vent. Eveleen let out a startled exclamation about the same moment he palmed his weapon and aimed it, flicking the safety off.

A figure slowly emerged, hands out-held.

They waited, not speaking, as the figure resolved in a humanoid form.

But the Baldy Ross expected failed to materialize. Instead, he stared at a being he'd only glimpsed once before, years ago on his very first run, at a station buried in ice: A triangular face, sharply pointed chin, angled jaw, small mouth, hooked nose. Dark skin covered with long, silky down, crest over the head, and below that two round eyes. Intelligent eyes.

The being slowly brought a furry hand to its chest and squawked in its high voice, using a language full of trills and clicks.

Moments later passable Greek emerged.

"You must come within, for I do not wish to cause you damage."

A small device glinted at them from the other hand and Ross realized it was some kind of weapon.

Chapter Nine

"You never married?" It was early—Eveleen and Ross were just past the oracle. The place was mostly empty but for the fallen greater buildings of Akrotiri, built haphazardly all along an axis, with the small rooms furnished with benches and bins and cubicles of stone.

Men did not have access to the buildings identified with the priestesses, only those that were made for general use or for men's concerns. Religion here was an integral as well as natural part of everyday life, as one could tell from the rise and fall of voices in song, the processions, the stylized clothing of various members of the religious callings. Women's rooms were not open to men, and Linnea went there alone, leaving Ashe to investigate those belonging to men only.

She had just emerged from one, wherein some local women were singing a lilting song as they decorated a young girl with flowers and a bright kilt, and last clasped a necklace of stylized serpents around her neck. On the walls was the famous fresco of the ladies, the flowers bright and fresh, the perspective breathtakingly graceful. A golden glow from oil lamps made the colors seem real.

Linnea had had to blink away tears. She had known what to expect, yet still she had not been really prepared for the effect of such free, bright, and generous beauty, and the corresponding claw of loss.

So she put her question about marriage to Ashe when she emerged, and he glanced at her, looking amused, and said, "No."

Just that word seemed bald, ungracious. She knew she had trespassed, even though she had taken care to use the Ancient Greek, not just to protect them, though no one paid them the least attention, but because its wording was necessarily quaint and distant from their habitual English, and so it created its own borders of finesse.

Then he added, as though he realized that he had sounded ungracious, "Though it was not an easy choice. But it seemed the best one. My absences would put a burden on a family."

She nodded. She had a brother in the military, and she knew what his wife had suffered when he would be gone one year, two, often without any communication. For twenty years she had spent holidays alone with their children, and birthdays, except for last-minute surprises; he had almost missed their daughter's wedding.

"You did not think to marry within the Project?"

"In the very early days there were few women. And I am, unfortunately, a member of the last generation. A wife with me would take my mind from the work to her, to protecting her. Though I know it's not fair, or right. But instinct is hard to argue with."

Linnea nodded. "Ross and Eveleen have managed."

"Many of the younger agents have paired off successfully, though not all the marriages last. They did not find it easy to adjust. Though they are much alike, and I believe they have an excellent chance of going the distance."

"Adventurers," Linnea said, the noun she chose calling to mind Homer and his tales.

They had emerged from one building and had tried another, but it was all fallen in, destroyed so badly that no one had even excavated the rubble yet. Either that or it had fallen relatively recently.

On to the next one, much smaller, roofed with woven mats. They peered in windows, watching people come and go. Though they could not examine every room, at least they could watch for anomalies.

The noon sun beat down, the air breathlessly hot, drifting with faint ash-fall. One of the tremors froze everyone for a moment into a tableau, a still life backlit by garish sun, while hissings of little stones sifted down from cracks in the walls.

Then songs rose again, donkeys brayed, children laughed, adults' voices exclaimed in question, concern, annoyance, worry, with many glances skyward up the mountain.

Linnea had just looked over to say something when the communicator Ashe wore next to his skin pulsed just once.

It was from the boat.

"An attack?" she spoke without thinking, but at least she'd used Ancient Greek.

He said nothing, of course, but nodded upward when they reached one of the narrow intersections. They toiled up a steep street, with a cliff to one side, looking down at roofs, some with withered gardens. Behind them were more buildings. As he left it to Linnea to peer in the windows and go into what buildings she could, he found a tiny join where one wall did not quite meet another, shaded by a very straggly wild palm. Trusting to its protection, Ashe raised to his eyes a slim pair of field glasses, shading them by his palm.

Linnea, seeing what he was about, backed out of his field of vision, instead watching the occasional passerby to draw attention away from Ashe if necessary.

She waited until his hand lowered.

"Baldies on the beach," he murmured.

Linnea felt her heart lurch.

They eased into a crowd moving down toward the shoreline, where the early morning fishers were just arriving in with fresh catch.

Linnea peered up along the sand, which seemed to shimmer in the heat. A thunderstorm was on the way, she realized, though judging from the faint, acid-tangy breeze and the slowness of those clouds, it would not arrive until sundown.

Ashe drew in a breath. He stepped aside from the street into an angle of the low wall that guarded the street from the sheer fall to the next level below. He leaned over, looking down, concealing his actions as he raised the glasses again, mostly covering them with his palm so it looked as if he were shading his eyes.

"I should have expected that," he murmured. "Right out in sight. Of course. People will see what they expect to see."

Silently he handed Linnea his glasses, and she copied his movement, covering them with her palm to shade her eyes as she scanned.

The shoreline seemed curiously flattened, colors muted. But there, not far from their anchorage (was that chance?), where the road from the city to the harbor passed close to the shore, there stood a group of slender hairless humanoids, all dressed alike in rich, glimmering fabric that changed from blue to green to purple depending on how the wearer moved.

The Kallistans walking past looked at them but did not linger or approach them. It was as though an invisible line were inscribed in the sand around them.

"I wonder if they have the same effect going as at that apparently abandoned building?" said Linnea in a bare whisper. "But what are they doing?"

For much of the time the Baldies did nothing, standing in silence, watching, as people streamed by. But occasionally, more often when the crowds moving between the city and the harbor were thickest, one of their number would step forward and stop a group of people. As they watched, the alien stopped a pair of young men.

The men looked up at the Baldy, their body language, even flattened by the distance, eloquent of fear and respect. The Baldy spoke, gestured; the men nodded and replied, then hurried away at a dismissive motion by the alien. The other Baldies paid no attention to the exchange, instead watching intently the people all around.

"They're looking for us."

"Or, if not us, anomalies among the people walking about?"

"They must know we won't expose ourselves in any way that the locals would notice," Ashe murmured, as around them, people exclaimed in worry about the poor catch and fishermen in approaching boats tried to gather crowds to them by calling out what was in their nets.

"How will we eat if the fish all die?" a woman exclaimed in Ancient Greek.

"No, they're probably not so much interested in the answers they get from people as in their reactions and those of the people around them," Ashe murmured. "We're not really clear on the capabilities and limitations of their suits, but I wouldn't be surprised if they could detect our subliminal awareness of who they are, the way we focus on them in a way different from the locals, who just think they're priests from some strange country."

Linnea nodded. That would certainly be true of an entrepôt like Kalliste, where people were used to strangers and wont to assume that any out-of-the-ordinary behavior could be ascribed to foreignness.

The women around them, waiting for the fishermen to unload their nets on the sand and spread out the fish, paid the two of them no attention.

"I think we are being punished," an older woman said.

"For what?" exclaimed the first. "I am a good wife; my husband is a good artisan; my children sing to the gods."

"But I think we'd have to be a lot closer," Ashe continued. "The Baldies cannot really control minds, or send messages, unless you wear their fabric, which has some sort of communication built in," Ashe murmured. "But they can certainly influence people, probably the more so when they're grouped together, as now. I'm sure there're some advanced statistics that guide the way they search. After all, time is on their side, no matter what they intend."

"It is the gods who fight one another," a third woman said, pointing up at the mountain.

"If they cast fiery stones at one another, it is we who are struck," said the first woman in a sour voice.

The older woman laughed. "It is always thus, in war."

Linnea sighed, cramping her fingers together in her robe. "What do we do?"

"Watch, wait, and keep a respectful distance."

Ash and Linnea spent most of the afternoon on or near the last set of stairs before the beach, watching. The Baldies remained where they were, somewhat down the road on the seaside, waiting with inhuman patience for the trace of an anachronistic mind.

Ashe watched them. Though he'd had many encounters with them over the years, this was the first sustained observation he had ever been able to make.

Linnea was quiet, obviously watching the volcano, the city, listening to the people, as Ashe walked and watched by turns. Late afternoon, after another of those long tremors, they followed a small boy herding baby goats up onto the rocky low hills adjacent to Akrotiri. The recent rains had brought up tufts of tough, brown-edged grasses through the ash and pumice drifts. The goats did not appear to like this grass and kept frolicking with one another as they sought green farther along.

Thus they passed up beyond the waiting Baldies, below on the shoreline, and then to the other side.

At last, as the oncoming clouds began to block the sinking sun, Linnea said, "They must think we are stupid."

Ashe shrugged. "Stupid? Ignorant is more like it. Remember, they know we have interfered with them, but they believe it is by accident. And they do not know where or when the humans who have opposed them come from. So as yet they have not interfered with us in our own time; we have managed to keep the time-lines safe."

Linnea frowned. Beyond her shoulder, over the edge of the headland, the sun was a crimson ball of fire underlighting the sky with spectacular, faintly sinister color. "So they think we're like the monkey with the typewriter, then?"

"I think so. We've worked hard to keep it that way. And to keep our encounters here in the past, where we originally found them."

"How strange, that beings who appear to be from the far future would be consistently discovered mucking about in the past."

"A mystery I've almost given up solving. It's enough to fend them off, to keep them from destroying us by tampering with the past," Ashe said. "Although, of course, that might be enough reason. Sort of flattering, really."

"What do you mean?"

"Well, maybe we're too strong, up in the future, and the only way they can attack us is in the past. But that begs the question: why attack us in the first place?"

Linnea shaded her eyes against the slanting ruddy glow of sunset, peering out through the forest of prows and masts of the incoming boats. "Do you suppose we'll ever know?"

Ashe shrugged.

Linnea sighed. "It was fortunate that Stav and Kosta went out hunting vents."

"I don't think the Baldies can find our boat, as long as they don't see anything to cause them to attack and investigate more closely," Ashe said.

Did he sound as doubtful as he felt?

"Our lab rats at home shielded the equipment fairly well in that boat; I doubt there's enough EM escaping to bring down alarms."

"Not over what must be emitting from there," Linnea said, looking up at the volcano.

"True—"

Ashe's words died when he saw the Baldies go tense and alert, their faces raised. Though no apparent signal was received, as one they set out at a fast pace, uphill, directly north.

Ashe thought of the attack on their camp, then looked at small Linnea, who had not had the time to get any sort of defense training. "Go on to your room and watch. Brief the others when they turn up," he said tersely. "I'm going to try to find the Baldies' base."

She did not argue. "Good luck."

Linnea hurried back toward the city gates by the lurid red light still glowing in the west. She still had plenty of lapis lazuli, but she did not want to waste one on a smelly, scarcely functional torch.

She was not the only person running to beat the oncoming darkness. Akrotiri at night glowed with dim but welcoming golden light, tiny pinpricks from uncounted lamps. She passed through the gates and ran the short way across the first market area toward her house.

By the light of the lamps many were still lingering over business; the day's heat was now just a stuffy sort of warmth and far more bearable. Linnea paused to trade for some grapes, more because she delighted in speaking with the people than for any other reason, and then bought a big bucket of water.

The bucket pulled at her shoulder joints, making her feel hotter than ever, and some sploshed out until she got the right rhythm for walking with it. Never again, she vowed, would she take for granted the infinite blessing of running water.

Of course some of the buildings had their own running water, even now, despite the quake destruction. She could hear and even smell it, a faintly sulfuric odor coming from an underground hot spring, but she had none in her little room.

And so she withdrew to it, and by the light of a swinging lamp coming weakly through the window opposite, she gave in to—oh, don't just call it temptation. The smell, the itchiness, of her underclothes had become so repulsive that washing them was now the first priority of her life.

She undressed under her robe, keeping well into the shadows of her room, though no one glanced in as people walked by. All the windows were open, and on the still, warm night air she could hear voices. She purified the water first, then drank. After that she washed her face and hands, and then her body as well as she could without completely undressing. And then she scrubbed her underthings. Since she had no soap, she scrubbed and rescrubbed until her hands felt red and tender, and the cloth smelled just like damp cloth. But where to put them?

She took the bucket out and splashed it into the gutter that ran downhill along the outer edge of the street. The bucket was to be returned in the morning. Until then, it was hers.

She draped the underclothes over the bucket, set it in the corner, and then lay down on the woven straw pallet that Eveleen had bought for them the night before. The dampness of her robe cooled her enough so that the very faint breeze felt pleasant.

Cooking smells wafted in, and the sounds of voices, so few now each was distinct: low laughter from across the way, a fretful child, a couple having an argument, all the more fierce for being whispered.

In the distance, far away, some voices began singing a song, the melody strange and yet curiously familiar, too. It pulled at the heart: a lament?

Linnea drifted into sleep.

When she woke, it was to the awareness of movement, of breathing. She looked up in dismay and amazement. Four women had crowded into her room, one of them being the bucket's owner.

One, a young woman in the tight jacket and flounced skirt of the prosperous, held up her camisole and underwear—the good cotton, machine-stitched underwear, and the fine cotton-silk camisole—and shook it at Linnea. She then made a demand in a language that was only vaguely familiar.

Chapter Ten

Linnea stared up at the women, her brain at first refusing to work. Was she dreaming? No, her neck was gritty, her mouth dry, and she realized she knew this language; the woman had spoken in Egyptian.

And now the women all looked at her with expressions ranging from curious to wary.

Wary.

What was it Gordon had said? There is no record of a woman speaking a foreign tongue, surprising people with things that never have been.

The woman frowned a little, then said again in her rough, stilted Egyptian, "Where got you these?"

Linnea thought rapidly, but another of the women forestalled her, saying in better Egyptian, "Why do you not trade this? You and the young one brought that old cloth from Kemt to trade, but our young girls make better." She turned her chin over her shoulder, making a spitting motion.

Curiosity was swiftly turning into hostility. *I am the stranger here*, Linnea thought, and she cleared her throat. "I wish we had such cloth to sell," she said. "Oh, how I have searched."

The women listened, the one's hostility easing slightly. "You tell us, then, that this is the only such things you have?"

"Yes," Linnea responded. "They were brought back for me by my man, from the Land of the Dragon, far, far in the direction of the morning sun."

"Ah," said the older women, all nodding.

"I have heard of that place," said the one with the jacket. "Some of the sailors have spoken of it. And the fine things that come from there, rare and precious. Precious enough for only the great families to trade precious artifacts of gold or very fine pearls."

Linnea, following instinct, said, "It is really for younger women, these fine things. You may have them, if you like."

The one with the jacket gaped in surprise and then pleasure. The youngest one gasped, running her fingers with reverence along the seams. "How tiny the threads are, how even. They must have looms the size of a cricket!"

"It is far too great a gift," said the older woman, and the one with the jacket flushed. "What can we offer you as a trade?"

In other words, why are you really here?

Linnea licked her lips, and because instinct had gotten her this far, she said tentatively, "I have come with my family to trade, but I myself have ... questions ... for your oracle. I know the priestesses where I live, and they said that I should consult over the seas," she added randomly.

The three older women nodded again, one with pursed lips. The youngest was still marveling over the machine stitching, holding the cloth only an inch or two from her eyes. Her big golden hoop earrings swung against her cheeks as she studied the seams.

"Ah yes, our oracle is renowned for her communion with the goddess; this we know. But we have troubled times, you can see," the oldest said, pointing toward the sky.

"I could ask about that, too," Linnea ventured, greatly daring.

"We do ask. Many ask each day, but there has been no answer."

"Perhaps it is for the far-sailing Kemtiu to break the silence?" asked the one with the jacket.

"Perhaps," agreed the oldest. And she made a gesture of decision. "I shall send you to the priestesses. My sister's girl is with them. Her name is Ela. Tell her that Theti sent you. She will gain you entrance on the mountain."

"That is a fair trade, is it not?" asked the one with the jacket.

There was no mistaking her anxious look. Linnea nodded. "I think it very fair."

The one with the jacket then plucked the garments from the younger woman, and vanished with a triumphant smile and a flounce of triply layered skirts.

Linnea was left to find her way to the communal toilets, under which ran a stream. She went straight out, bought some fresh flatbread and cheese, and then started up the mountain to find Ela, and the oracle.

At the same time, Ross and Eveleen woke up, surrounded by complete darkness.

Ross fought the instinct to panic and forced himself to lie still, to mentally review.

He remembered reaching the summit. Remembered the great vent and Eveleen taking pictures of the inner waters, before stashing her camera back in her clothing. He remembered turning around, and there was the Fur Face.

It used some kind of translator to gabble some idiocy about not damaging them while holding a weapon pointed their way.

So they'd gone within, into the heat and dangerous fumes. A smoothed passage then, made by very high-tech means, after which they were motioned into this chamber and the door shut, cutting off all light.

Eveleen had not reacted at all, other than to hold his hand. He'd squeezed her hand in warning, and she'd squeezed back: *I know what to do.*

What to do? Locking people up in a room to wait was a standard scare tactic, meant to soften up prisoners, make them really sweat about their fate. Darkness made it worse. What's more: if there were two, they were only left together in hopes that someone, unseen, would get to overhear talk.

So they'd stayed silent, after a time stretching out on the stone floor and catching up on their rest.

Now Ross was awake, and from the sound of her changed breathing, Eveleen was as well. He groped about and found her hand. He spelled into her palm, *See or hear anything?*

Not a thing. It feels like morning.

I think so, too. I'll bet we'll see action soon.

He didn't want to speculate what kind.

While Ross and Eveleen waited, and Linnea Edel slowly trudged up the mountain path, on the northern shore of the peninsula that formed one end of their island-crescent, Gordon Ashe woke up, bleary-eyed and headachy.

He looked around. No sign of the Baldies—of course.

Damn.

Down in a little gully to his left he saw some goats drinking from a small stream. He swallowed convulsively. The stream appeared to be bubbling up from underground, which meant it was probably sanitary. He had certainly risked worse during his many runs; he did have massive antibiotic doses back at the ship, but meantime his canteen was empty, and he had to get some water. He worked his way down the rocky incline. The goats scattered, the older ones scolding him with an insistent "*Na-ha-ha-ha!*"

The water tasted faintly metallic. It had to be rich in minerals, but there was no dangerous flatness as of rotting matter or other pollutants. He drank his fill, and then sat down to think.

He'd followed the Baldies at a respectable distance, not knowing how far their supposed detection might range. But they had not once looked back as they sped in a group northward over the hills. Ashe had followed, using all his years of experience at outdoor trail-craft to stay silent and out of sight but still keep them within his vision. Yet even so, just as the moon rose, he lost them.

He could hardly be blamed. He been edging along a crumbling section of the trail, the Baldies just ahead around a turn, when a sudden quake sent the trail underfoot hurtling down toward the dry creek bed far below.

The next ninety or so nearly vertical feet were like surfing on dirt; Ashe frantically pedaled his feet, keeping himself on top of the swirling dirt and rocks as the mass slid ever faster downward. He was successful until just a couple of feet from the bottom, when a larger rock banged into the back of his knee and sent him sprawling. The impact knocked the breath out of him; he grayed out for a moment. The agent was dimly aware of more rocks hitting him, then silence broken only by random slippages of pebbles.

When he scrambled back to the trail, he hurried forward, limping, finally catching a glimpse of the Baldies far ahead. But only once. He soon was forced to conclude that he'd lost them. The trail was hard and stony there, and he could find no footprints.

By the light of the low-hanging moon he had grimly worked his way from that spot in ever widening circles, but not a trail, or cave, or door did he find. So he'd finally laid himself down on a grassy little hillock to sleep.

Now that it was daylight, he was determined to do another search, and if he did not find any suspicious anomalies like indications of spaceship burn, evidence of vehicle tracks, or flattened vegetation in the case of something air cushioned, he'd be forced to give up and return to the ship empty-handed.

He got to his feet, pulled the stale remains of his flatbread from the leather pouch at his waist, and chewed as he started his search.

It did not surprise Eveleen that Ross's instincts were right.

With a hiss of muted hydraulics a crack of light appeared, rapidly widening into a doorway. Ross and Eveleen blinked, trying to adjust to the light. She put her hands up to her face, discovered her breathing mask. Panic! With a few more exchanges spelled out on each other's palms, they'd decided to stick to their covers. They hastily adjusted the cloth covering their faces and heads, so only their eyes showed and the breathing masks stayed hidden.

She cast a look Ross's way, and he gave his head a tiny shake.

The doorway darkened. One of the Fur Faces appeared, gesturing for them to come out. Another was in view behind. They slowly rose to their feet. Eveleen watched Ross look around as though totally mesmerized. His gaze, she saw with a bleak spurt of amusement, lingered on how the door retracted into the rock and the mechanism that controlled it.

Out they walked. The two Fur Faces closed in behind them, tall, dressed in shapeless robes, each carrying something short and tubular in a clawed, double-jointed hand. Another Fur Face stepped in front of them, blocking off what had to be some kind of computer console, an egg of shimmering metal and misty bars of light, shapes that trembled in constant motion.

She and Ross were guided into another room, this one light, with another partially blocked off console. The Fur Faces prodded them not ungently back toward the wall and then lined up behind the console.

A Fur Face did something; they could not see what from their angle. The machine hummed, then spoke in a metallic, flat voice: "Who are you, and what seek you on the mountain?" The language was Ancient Greek.

Ross cleared his throat. "We are Timos and Hesti, and we came in search of our missing goat."

One of the Fur Faces spoke softly into what had to be their equivalent of a pin mike. This time the question came out in what sounded very much like Ancient Egyptian.

Eveleen felt a flare of danger. So the Fur Faces did not believe their pose? Would they rip off the breathing masks, then? The virtual overlay in her mask indicated that the chamber was filled with dangerous levels of hydrogen sulfides—natural to volcanoes and also, apparently, to Fur Faces.

They stayed silent, and a moment later, the machine spoke again, in a guttural language that sounded vaguely like Ancient Norse. Then once more, this time in some prehistoric form of Goth or Visigoth.

Eveleen did her best to seem bewildered, though inside she felt a spurt of relief. Even if the Fur Faces did not believe that they were bona fide Kallistans, at least they appeared to believe that she and Ross were from the ancient world.

Her relief was short-lived. The next language to emerge from that machine was Classical Latin. And then the machine proceeded through a remarkable, no, an intimidating number of languages, Eastern and Western, right up until modern times. When it spat out the same question in English—*Who are you? Why are you here?*—and then in German, French, Russian, Japanese, and Chinese, Eveleen had time to consider the fact that modern times were not, as they had comfortably surmised, unknown to these aliens.

After that the machine went on to speak in strange amalgams of what might be English and other languages. Eveleen thought that these would be a linguist's joy to hear, but they were so much gibberish to her, familiar yet not.

She'd just finished that thought when the Fur Face halted the stream of questions.

Silence, as the Fur Face fumbled at the console.

Eveleen was distracted by a warning pressure on her hand, which Ross still held. He pinched her little finger, tugging it to the right.

The right?

She looked up, just as the Fur Face's machine said, again in Ancient Greek, "There are two tongues here that make your blood-organ speed its rate of pumping—"

And before it could identify English, Ross drew in a sharp breath. That was the only warning Eveleen had. As

Ross launched himself to the left, she whirled to the right, launching a high kick, a snap to the Fur Face's narrow jaw. As it staggered off balance she gave it a knuckle blow to what would be the solar plexus on a human, and the being crumpled soundlessly to the stone floor. She bent, relieved that she had judged right: the Fur Face was still breathing.

Ross's groaned, but then subsided into unconsciousness.

Eveleen held her hands up, waiting for the other two to attack, and then stared: they stood, impassive, their sight focused on the wall where the two Time Agents had been standing.

Then it dawned on her. "Holographs?" she whispered.

He nodded, raised a finger to his lips.

Of course. The machine had to be recording whatever was said.

They both sprang to the console, which was of course totally incomprehensible. Ross scanned it and then began pressing pads and lights, and when the machine responded with flickers and streams of glyphs, he pressed more pads and lights, then stepped back and delivered a vicious chopping kick down onto the console. There was a musical jangling from within the egg, and several indicators changed color or went dark. Ross kept at it, obviously hoping to at least confuse things.

Then they moved to the door. Eveleen reached for the control mechanism; the door slid open, and they were in the outer room. No one around.

She chanced a word. "Weapon?" She used Ancient Greek.

Ross shook his head. "Useless." He answered in the same tongue.

He paused long enough to do the same thing to the console out there, and then they ran to what had to be the outer door. Again it slid open almost silently, and the two ran up the smoky stone vent to the surface.

"Let's get out of here," Ross said, and they plunged down the path.

Chapter Eleven

By the time Ross and Eveleen reached the harbor, the day was ending. Four rolling quakes and a brief, fierce thunderstorm full of stinging acid rain had slowed them, but at last they arrived just as the boat sailed up and dropped anchor.

Ross looked around and saw Gordon Ashe coming down the hard-packed trail from Akrotiri.

"Looks like we all had the same idea," Gordon greeted Ross.

"I wish we didn't have to stick with radio silence," Ross said.

Gordon gave his head a shake.

Before he could speak, Ross said, "I know; I know. Baldies could listen in, and identify our time-frame as well as where we are. But you didn't know this. The Baldies are not our only problem."

And, as Stavros and Kosta came up to join them, Ross gave a swift report on his and Eveleen's experiences inside the volcano.

The others listened in tense silence.

Ross finished, "...I watched the Fur Faces while the language test was going on and realized that two of them were damn still for supposedly live beings. Only two of them reacted. Then I watched those weapons, or what we thought were weapons. No firing stud or trigger or anything made me wonder if they were just pointing a handy piece of tech at us, their equivalent of a camera or something, and letting us provide the imaginary firepower. So when they started to tell us that our heart rates had given us away, I figured it was time for do or die. Signaled to Eveleen, and we jumped them."

Ashe turned Eveleen's way. She obviously interpreted his look before Ross could, and said, "We left them unconscious."

"We also did our best to mess up their computer setup, which looked field-rigged; then we hightailed out."

"Holographs," Ashe said, looking grim. "I didn't think of that. And I thought the trail they were leaving was a little thin."

Everyone looked at him.

Ashe sighed, and said, "Linnea and I spent most of yesterday watching a group of Baldies standing right out in the open, occasionally interrogating people. That is, only a couple of them did; the rest just watched. When they suddenly took off, I followed them. A quake knocked me over a bit of a cliff, and when I was able to follow, they had gotten too far ahead, and I lost them. But I realize now their trail didn't look right, so maybe some of them were holos and I ended up following a bunch of phantoms."

"*Moving* holos?" Ross asked, scratching his itchy scalp.

Ashe shrugged a shoulder. "Considering the sophisticated level of the rest of their tech, it's entirely possible. A moving projector should be easy enough, if they have a strong enough power source."

Eveleen said soberly, "If you're right, it would indicate that they don't have huge numbers. Not if they have to go to the trouble of falsifying their head count."

"Exactly," Ashe said. "Might even the odds a bit."

"You think they knew you were following them?" asked Eveleen.

"No." He shook his head. "They would have tried to capture me; even with holos they had me outnumbered. I think it was standard procedure to throw off anyone following them. I'll bet they can hide behind holos of the surroundings as well—a perfect way to hide the opening to their base."

"So we can't find it that way."

"Probably not, and anyone poking around that far out from the city would automatically alert them."

"They'll be back," Ross said. "After all, what they're trying to do is flush us out."

"At least, so we guess," Stavros put in. "So far, we ascribe human motivations and reactions to them."

"Oh, they've been human enough in some of their reactions in the past," Ross stated in a grim voice. "Those boys don't play nice, not at all."

"No, they don't," Ashe said. "But we still do not know what game they are playing. Not really."

"My question," Kosta said, wiping back dark curly hair from his brow, "is, are these *Younoprosopoi* their allies, or enemies?"

"A good question, one I'd like an answer to myself," Ashe said.

Eveleen smiled. "I like that. *'Younoprosopoi.'* Is that Modern Greek? It sounds a little like our present Kallistan Greek."

Kosta flashed a grin. "Means 'Fur Faces.' "

Ross said, "Since I was until now the only one who'd ever seen one of these guys, and that was during an attack that we decided later was some sort of triple cross involving the

Russians, the Baldies, and at least one Fur Face, what they're doing here is anybody's guess."

"Then let's continue to gather facts. Stav, Kosta. What did you find over at the pre-Kameni Island?"

"Evidence of at least six of those devices, all buried very deeply."

"Did you mark them?"

"We have got markers floating over each," Kosta said.

"Good. Then tomorrow we need to find out if they are in the nearer vents."

"More area to cover," Stav said.

"Start today, then. Take all night."

"I'll go with them," Eveleen offered. "I haven't been on a dive for, oh, a whole six months. I hate to get out of practice."

"An excellent idea." Ashe smiled a little.

Then he turned to Ross, who said first, "You thinking what I'm thinking?"

Ashe shrugged. "I think it's time for some desperate measures. I do not condone undue violence, but perhaps our *Younoprosopoi* friends will not resist our invitation for a little talk."

Stav looked a little confused.

Eveleen said, "Where is Linnea?"

"I was just looking for her," Ashe said. "Before I spotted you coming down the trail and hiked down to meet you here. Answer: I don't know. She was not at that little room you two rented."

"Invitation?" Stav murmured, still looking confused. "Invitation? Is this an idiom with which I am not familiar?"

"No," Eveleen said, casting him a distracted look. "Linnea must be off investigating something," she said. "I can go check, just in case. Maybe one of those women there saw her."

"A good idea," Ashe said, still studying the volcano under its pall of smoke, as if he could see a small figure toiling up and down the trail. "In case whatever she's on the track of requires backup."

"What is this 'invitation'?" Stav asked Ross.

Ross sent a tight grin Ashe's way and then said to the Greek agent, "We're going to do a little alien-napping."

Chapter Twelve

Linnea heard the singing first.

She emerged onto the cliff outside the oracle's cave, tired and sweaty, to the faint smell of sulfur and the sound of young girls' voices.

The voices rose and fell in a strange chant. It wasn't music, not to a modern, Western-trained ear, but nor was it totally dissonant.

Mesmerizing, Linnea thought, already mentally writing her monograph... except where could she publish it? Project Star was totally secret. She then realized something she had, so far, avoided looking at: that Gordon Ashe, with his fine mind and eternal curiosity, had never published anything. Yet how many fabulous secrets of the human past had he seen?

What does he do? Linnea thought as she crossed the cliff and stood with the little cluster of waiting people. Does he plant clues so that other archaeologists can find them the customary way? Or does he live with the knowledge of treasures of knowledge permanently suppressed?

Or is the word *permanently* an arrogant assumption? One thing for certain, he had long ago accepted that fame would not be his. (Never mind fortune. Archaeologists don't get rich, even if they are lucky enough to uncover vast quantities of gold and precious gems in rich tombs; governments then thud in with their heavy feet, waving official papers right and left, leaving archaeologists with little but their dwindling stipend and the hopes that they can get credit for their find.)

So, if a trained mind like his had given up the idea of fame, what was the payoff? The satisfaction of a job well done?

That sounds noble but not quite human, *Linnea thought, smiling.*

A teenage girl dressed in a brightly colored robe, with a golden necklace of stylized serpents, looked up into Linnea's face. She said something—asked a question.

Linnea suppressed the urge to write down the girl's speech and compare it to Greek as the girl then restated in careful Ancient Greek, "Your quest?"

"I seek Ela," Linnea said in the same Ancient Greek, trying to match accents. "Theti sent me."

"Sent you? Why?"

"I met her in Akrotiri," Linnea explained, and then she offered the cover she'd invented on the long walk uphill. "I am a priestess of the Earth Goddess, only from Kemt. I was sent by the goddess to witness here."

And the girl took it without a blink. "You must come within," she said, gesturing. "We are still finishing the purification, so—" She touched a forefinger to her lips and led the way past the waiting petitioners, who watched with patient attitudes, and curious eyes.

Linnea followed, feeling morally queasy at how easily her lie had been believed. She had always assumed that those who lived around oracles made their living by listening to gossip. Did they really accept directives from outside, just on the word of someone claiming to be sent by their deity?

At least I intend no harm, Linnea thought. *I will do nothing but observe and learn what I may. And my mission is to save these people from a really horrible fate.*

The smell of sulfur intensified as they eased past a great crack between two massive rocks. Short as she was, Linnea had to duck and walk sideways for several yards, until cool air suddenly ruffled against her face and they emerged into a wide cavern with a sudden drop at the left. Linnea did not have to look down to see the rushing water. Above the stream, far above, was another great crack. A shaft of faint golden light, widening slowly, filtered in.

A circle of young girls, all in brightly colored robes with red jackets edged with blue, walked with deliberate step in a circle round what looked like an ancient tree stump, their arms upraised, fingers brought to a point like a beak—or like the head of a serpent, Linnea realized, as she watched the sinuous, dancelike swayings and pouncings of those young arms and hands.

Linnea transferred her gaze to the center of the circle. Had a tree really once grown here? Well, there was light, and below ran water. All that was needed was some bird to drop a seed while flying over that crack.

As the thin shaft of light crept closer to the great tree, Linnea perceived movement in the shadows at the other end of the cave, beyond the circle of the girls and the tree.

Ching! Ching! A girl clashed little copper cymbals, and the chant began again. Between the young bodies, swaying in unison as the girls' voices rose, faintly echoing, Linnea glimpsed a shadowy form all in red.

Two steps, three, and the form resolved into a woman, an older woman, spare of build, her sparse hair bound up in a golden serpent-fillet like those of the girls, her eyes dark and surrounded by wrinkles.

Two older women assisted her. When she neared the circle the young girls did not break their step, only amended it, creating a gap, through which the old woman came on alone.

She approached the great tree stump and climbed up onto it. Linnea couldn't quite see the cut portion, as it was about five feet from the rocky floor, but there seemed to be a seat carved in it, for the priestess sat, just as a thin finger of sunlight touched her hair, lighting the gray to molten silver and shrouding her face in shadow.

The girls finished their chant on a triumphant note and filed back down the narrow crevasse through which Linnea had come. Moments later the sound of the voices floated back: now, apparently, the purification ritual included the petitioners outside.

The priestess sat in her tree-stump throne, breathing slowly, her eyes closed, her hands lying palms up and open on her knees.

Presently a woman walked in, looking about a little fearfully. Her eyes lifted to the great shaft of light, which now fully illuminated the priestess on the throne.

Good theater, Linnea thought, but the skin along her outer arms felt rough.

"Mother Goddess," the woman said in Ancient Greek, as she mounted the gnarled tree roots and joined the seer on the stump. "O Mother Goddess, why do the crops fail, and the sky fill with smoke, and the ground growl at us like a beast hunting prey? What can we do?"

The priestess did not answer. Her eyes stayed closed. A soft hissing sound emerged from the cone of brilliant sunlight, and Linnea realized it was the seer's breathing. Those breaths were long, each slightly louder than the one before, a hiss that sounded very like a snake.

A snake. Just as Linnea identified the sound, the seer straightened up. She seemed to grow, to expand a little, as she lifted her face up toward the sunlight. Still the hissed breathing, in and out, and Linnea became aware of the older priestesses standing along the perimeter of the chamber breathing in the same slow rhythm.

Then, slowly, the seer began to sway, reminding Linnea of the snakelike swayings of the girls during the purification chants. Her head turned from side to side, almost like a blinded snake looking, seeking, reaching. Listening.

Linnea, realizing that, felt prickles again, but she caught herself up, thinking, *This is just theater. It's good theater—the very best—but it's all showmanship.*

Still, it was three-thousand-year-old showmanship, and as such, it was very well worth watching. And she forced herself to divert from the hindbrain's awe by counting up the elements, one by one, that made the whole seem so unnervingly... *real.*

The far-off girls' voices, chanting in a mesmerizing pattern; the light; the great aged tree stump that had grown so unlikely in this cavern; the rushing water; even the faint whiffs of sulfur. And then the old seer's rhythmic writhing: despite her evident age, she moved now, graceful and supple as one of those young acolytes out front.

At last she spoke, in a voice that startled Linnea. It was a guttural voice, harsh, loud, and because it was in the local language (or was it?) she could not understand a word.

But the petitioner appeared to understand, for she bowed her head, and her tense shoulders slumped.

A priestess moved forward to help her down, and she walked out slowly, her face drawn and worried.

Linnea turned to the nearest priestess, who saw her movement and touched her fingertips to her lips.

One by one the rest of the petitioners came in, and again and again the seer breathed that hissing breath and writhed, her eyes wide open but blind-looking. Again she cried out something in that guttural voice that clawed at Linnea's viscera, and the petitioners departed in silence, not one of them looking happy with the answers that they got.

There were seven of them. If others waited outside, they had been dismissed. The sun had moved, in the meantime, and the golden shaft now left the seer on her throne and painted the rocky floor instead. The seer, in shadow, seemed to shrink in on herself, and without any words spoken two sturdy middle-aged priestesses moved to the sides of the great tree to help her down.

Her eyes were open, but she seemed to be blind. Her hands, once graceful, now fumbled, looking frail and aged.

The priestesses all moved around the empty tree and followed the seer into that back area. Linnea hesitated, and then joined them, moving tentatively, but no one shooed her away or otherwise paid attention to her.

They each ducked under a triangular archway made by two slabs of pumice cracked and shifted apart by unimaginable forces, and Linnea found herself in a back chamber. It was stuffy here; there was no sky-crack to let in air. Reflected light from the tree chamber was dim, revealing rugs on the ground.

The seer was gently helped onto one of these. Everyone stood in silence as she stretched out, breathing slowly again, but without that awful hiss.

After a time she stirred, made a motion to sit, and again two priestesses sprang to help her, their movements tender with unspoken love and respect.

Someone brought in a little oil lamp and set it down before the seer. Its tiny tongue of flame painted golden color on a worn face that now looked sweet, grandmotherly, and very, very weary.

"Thirst," she murmured—in Ancient Greek.

Someone brought her a cup of water, probably from the stream. Someone else brought dried fish and crumbled goat cheese, and a tiny bunch of withered grapes.

The seer munched her way through these foods with no apparent enjoyment. Her brow was slightly puckered, as if she had a massive headache, and she chewed and swallowed as one performing a duty.

At last the food was gone, and all of the water. She sighed, and one of the women gently massaged her temples.

No one spoke, not until one of the girls came in and said, "Maestra, they are all gone."

The woman who had brought the water turned her head. "Thank you, child. Tell the others they are free to eat their meal."

Others among the priestesses stirred now, some passing out fava-seed bread, cheese, grapes. The priestesses talked in low murmurs as the seer had her head rubbed, her eyes closed now. She was surrounded by quiet now, as before she'd been surrounded by that fierce shaft of bright sunlight, the more fierce, Linnea realized, because of all the particulate matter in the air. The sun here before the volcano began smoking and rumbling must have been pure and clear, as clear as the ocean waters.

At last the seer looked up. Her question was the last thing Linnea expected: "What did I say?"

And the chief priestess shook her head sadly. "Nothing. The spirits are still silent."

Chapter Thirteen

"Up this way," Ross said, pointing.

He paused, gazing up the mountain path. A wisp of smoke haze drifted by, borne on the strengthening breeze. The smoke seemed to leech all the color out of the sparse hillside, rendering it unfamiliar, almost alien.

"Or was it?"

"Can you orient on the peninsula?" Ashe asked, after a time.

Ross felt a hot zap of annoyance at his own stupidity. Yes, the smoke had given him a fairly nasty headache, making it difficult to think, but Ashe probably had one as well.

Ross turned around, staring down through the haze toward the peninsula that stretched westward from below Akrotiri. The pre-Kameni Island was barely visible through the murk of smoke and steam, but one thing he could see was the purple clouds headed their way. Even if he hadn't felt fitful puffs of cooler, moisture-laden air pushing through the hot, humid haze, he would have sensed a major storm on the way. From the tightness at the base of his skull, the way the hairs on his arms prickled, it was a storm that carried a full load of artillery in the form of lightning and hail.

"We're going to have to find cover," he said to Ashe.

The man shrugged. "Let's get as high as we can. Maybe dive into some crevasse if we don't find your vent first."

Ross nodded once, ignoring the corresponding pang in his head, and turned around again. He remembered orienting himself several times on that previous journey. "Yes. That way," he said, pointing up to the left.

They trudged on.

The storm came on with energetic rapidity.

Eveleen and Kosta dropped over the side of the boat away from the coast, so that no one who happened to have field glasses, or the alien equivalent, would see their scuba gear. Stav had erected a tent onboard, which was common enough, especially when the weather was as fierce as it was now.

They unclipped the sled from the hull of the boat and hung on as the small but powerful electric motor pulled them away and down. A strong sense of relief shot through Eveleen as they moved steadily downward. The wind had been getting up, and the water had formed little whitecaps; though they couldn't see beyond the mountain blocking the northern sky, Stav had said with Greek stoicism, "Storm on the way. I'll batten down once you two get under the surface."

Out this far from any others they could speak English, which was a relief. Though the Greek agents still called the mysterious Fur Faces *Younoprosopoi*, and they also called the Baldies *Falakri*, or *Exoyinii*. Eveleen found these nicknames more elegant, even though the first one simply meant "bald ones" and the second "aliens." The sobriquet "Baldies" for the hairless aliens of the future sounded kind of silly, but it had stuck over decades. *Rather like the way we still call Native Americans "Indians,"* Eveleen thought as she swam downward, laughing inside. *Which probably thoroughly confuses any aliens who spy in our time.*

The light changed abruptly. They'd reached the level where shafts shifted and changed, but suddenly they faded and vanished. Eveleen flipped over, holding on to the sled with one hand, and saw the remarkable effect of hail and rain pockmarking the surface. It was a beautiful sight, but she forced herself to turn back. *Some day,* she resolved, *if we get back all right, I will have time to watch a storm from below.*

Next to her Kosta turned on his forehead lamp and started surveying the depths in its beam.

Eveleen turned hers on as well and then pulled out the device that Ashe had given her. They couldn't use sonics for this search; there was too much area to be covered and the returns were confused by the water. Ashe's device wasn't much better, but it worked underwater. About all it could do was detect the presence of alien tech within a range of twenty yards; as one might expect when dealing with a technology far beyond most theories contemporary scientists could come up with, it could tell little more. But after much research, and the invention of a different way of looking at quantum mechanics, the brain boys had realized that the power source for Baldie tech involved some sort of temporal distortion, and some smart lab jockey had figured a way to use a piece of the Baldies' own tech to home in on its brethren via that signature. Unfortunately, it was active detection, so they were announcing themselves to the Baldies by using it. But that couldn't be helped. At least they knew where they were—and maybe their actions were causing the devices to be turned off. That was enough, for now.

She and Kosta reached the cliffs supporting the island. Dramatic striations of rock and great upthrusts of ancient pumice testified to the terrific volcanic activity of the past millions of years.

She flicked her device on and held it out. A faint signal responded, pretty much the same signal the men had gotten on their first preliminary cruise.

Now to get a vector on position.

Kosta took the sled—he was far more practiced in its use, and it was difficult to steer when it was going slowly. Eveleen swam away from him until they were just in sight of each other. She checked the detector: still a good signal, if weak.

She turned Kosta's way and saw him gesture toward his device, confirming that he, too, still had a signal.

By hand signals they divided up the immediate terrain, and Kosta dove down to explore parallel to Eveleen. They would continue to do so until their air ran low, occasionally syncing the machines for a pattern comparison that, they hoped, would locate any Baldie tech.

Curious fish swam slowly by as they proceeded along the silent rock face with its dotting of colorful plants. Eveleen looked at those plants with their astonishing variety of waving fronds, tentacles, and cilia, and frowned, thinking of what was going to happen to them all before long. These were the plants that scientists would eventually find fossilized by burning lava three thousand years up the line.

She shook her head. Plenty of time to brood later.

A faint flash of purple caused her to roll over. Another flash of purple beyond the surface, which was otherwise quite dark, gave evidence of a truly violent storm going on.

Eveleen turned back to work. They proceeded along the rock face for an hour, Kosta zooming over to her every fifteen minutes to link the devices, just to discover that the detectors still couldn't localize the signal. Strange. Eveleen watched her device. Either it was defective or it was insufficiently sensitive.

A faint signal without locale... could that mean bits of low-end tech all over? Or was it the opposite? A great concentration of alien tech, but at a remove?

A little while longer, and she started checking her tank every ten minutes. About four checks later, Kosta maneuvered the sled up to her, indicating that this was the place they were to go up. He had the compass, and they'd planned out the exploration with Stav in the boat.

They arrowed up. Eveleen was relieved to see that the color of the sky was once again blue, that the surface was visible.

Her relief was short-lived.

When they popped up and removed their masks, Stav and the boat were nowhere in sight.

Linnea watched the water shaft down through the crack in the ceiling as the priestesses went about their business. The girls, given permission, danced about in the waterfall, cooling themselves off. They giggled and splashed water on one another, so much like girls of modern times—like Linnea's own daughter had at that age. The sight smote her heart. *We have to save them*, she thought. And again, *Why am I here?*

So far, she had found out exactly nothing.

The storm had come on fast. As the seer sat in silent meditation, the women finished their meal and set about cleaning up the few remains.

Now some of them took off their robes and washed them in the waterfall from the rain, then stepped into the water.

Judging from their reaction, it was cool but not miserable. They gasped, but with delight.

Linnea, itchy, gritty, gave in to impulse. She couldn't bring herself to disrobe completely. Old conditioning was too strong for that. But she could get herself and her robe soaked, and at least wash away most of the sweaty grime.

The women, unconcerned, chattered around her. Linnea turned her face up into the water, which had run long enough to be free of silt. As the refreshing coolness pounded down onto her, she gasped, and then as the aggravating itchy heat dissipated, replaced by a sense of cool cleanliness, her mind ranged freely, and she thought about the day.

It was no longer fair to even think "theater," she had decided. These women were not pulling a scam, however other oracles and cults had worked in other times and places. They sincerely believed in what they were doing; there was no reason to behave the way they did otherwise. They were also obviously not stupid people. In their paradigm, what they believed made sense.

How to speak to them so that she would not disturb their worldview but convince them to listen, perhaps to evacuate?

For a brief time she considered faking her own "seeing," but she thought of the perceptive gaze of that old woman sitting so motionlessly in the stifling inner room, and shook her head. She might not be hearing her "spirits" now, but she'd know a phony when she saw one.

Linnea realized her fingers and toes were slowly growing numb and she stepped out of the waterfall, which was now tapering off in intensity. The storm was passing.

When Linnea was dry again, several of the girls, who had been whispering off to one side, approached her. Some looked timid, others frankly curious.

"Please, tell us about faraway Kemt?" one asked.

"What must the girls do there to become priestesses?" asked a second.

A third, blushing and giggling, said, "Are they permitted to talk to young men?"

The first two gasped and shushed her.

Ela stepped up then, before Linnea could scrape her memory for some likely details of Ancient Egypt. She looked from Linnea to the girls and said, in a kind but firm voice, "Is this the way we treat a guest?"

The girls looked abashed.

"You must permit our visitor to speak of her home and customs in her own time."

The girls murmured, one in disappointment, the rest in apology.

"The people will be gone," said one of the older priestesses, coming to join the group. "We will have some sunlight left in which to dry your things. Take them outside."

The girls vanished toward the plateau, and Linnea walked around the tree-throne, touching the ancient, gnarled wood lightly with her fingers.

A little while later, the girls came trooping back in, chattering, some fussing with their hair, others smoothing sun-dried robes.

The light was fading, Linnea realized. She had tried to form up facts in a logical manner, but the truth was she was here on instinct.

Well, she had wool-gathered too long, unproductive as it had been. The sun was fast vanishing, and she did not want to find herself in total darkness on that narrow path down the mountain, especially after such a rain. She could slip and fall and no one would know.

"Come." Ela was there, smiling. "It is time for the evening meal, and our thanksgiving."

The girls had gathered and began another of their chants as fava breads were passed around, and dried fish that had been cooked in olives, and cheese and dates. Others lit the little oil lamps, which cast a weak but cozy golden glow.

All the women chanted, their voices, old and young, musical and unmusical, blending pleasingly. When they were done the seer began to eat, which was the signal for the others to begin their meal. The younger girls all withdrew to a far corner, whispering in the manner of young adolescent girls the world over. Occasional giggles escaped, skipping back in light echoes.

After she ate, Linnea found a comfortable place in which to sit and observe.

Across the cave two women set up a loom, and Linnea watched the rhythmic motions of their hands. It was oddly soothing; though the light was poor, a faint gold that rendered the scene almost dreamlike, the women were obviously so accustomed to their work that their fingers knew what to do while their eyes gazed, distant, at the little lamps, or the two conversed in soft voices.

Three of the younger girls picked up big fans plaited out of some fibrous plant and waved them, forcing the hot, stuffy air to circulate. Presently a touch of cool breeze, smelling of water, caressed Linnea's damp face.

Her eyelids drifted down, and since no one seemed to object, she stretched out on one of the cloth pads and slept.

Ross and Ashe found a cave just before the hail struck with such force it cracked little rocks from the cliffside and sent them tumbling down the mountain into an unseen gully below. Lightning struck all over the mountaintop as the storm roared and thundered.

Finally there was the hiss of rain, and both stepped out to cool themselves off and to drink. The rain was so heavy Ross only had to stand there with his eyes shut and his mouth open, and swallow and swallow.

The storm departed as swiftly as it had come, leaving the pathway up dangerously slippery. Here and there mudslides had peeled away at the path. With a sickening lurch Ross felt his foot start to slide, and leaped back just in time; a portion of the pathway crumbled, sloughing down a sheer cliff face.

Neither man spoke. They stuck closer to the mountain and kept toiling upward, until the light had faded in the west and it was too dangerous to continue.

They found some shelter under a rock overhang, squatted down in the mud, and tried their best to sleep.

Ross was in a vile mood when he woke. He itched all over, and the sight of steam rising gently off the mud outside their overhang promised a day even hotter than the one before.

They toiled up a little farther and presently decided they'd better put on their breathing masks.

They did, feeling much better immediately. They set out at a more energetic pace or at least began to set out.

Ross froze when he saw the tall figure standing near a familiar outcropping of rock, a patient stance, as if the being had long been waiting and watching.

"You seek me?" it said, in English.

Chapter Fourteen

Ross had just enough presence of mind not to answer. A long pause ensued, during which no one moved, or spoke, and then the being said in Ancient Greek, "You seek me?"

Ross turned to Gordon in question: do we take this guy prisoner or not? And Gordon looked back, brows raised.

The alien's hands were empty. The other one of its kind was nowhere in sight.

"Let's talk," Ross said, indicating slightly higher ground. Neutral ground, away from caves full of mysterious tech.

In answer the being walked round smoke-withered shrubs, rocks crunching underfoot. Ross, feeling uneasy, followed that long robe with its dusty hem, and Gordon fell in behind him.

For a short time the alien looked out over the vista. Smoke and haze diffused the horizon, but Ross, scanning fast, made out smoke plumes issuing from the mountain maybe a mile or two to the north and a twin plume lazily rising from the pre-Kameni Island out in the great lagoon. The island was just barely a silhouette in the yellow-tinged murk.

"Who are you?" Ross demanded.

Gordon half-raised a hand, and Ross clamped his mouth shut, folding his arms across his chest. *Shut up*, he thought.

They've already half-guessed what time we really come from. Don't hand them any more clues.

The alien's speech was tenor and softly sibilant, almost whistling; though the face and body were vaguely humanoid, its palate sounded like it was constructed differently.

"Call uss Kayu."

Gordon replied, "Why are you here?"

"We are here to halt our old enemiess, if we can. We are now two only. Time," the Kayu added, as a hot, stinging breeze ruffled through its silky hair, "iss dessperate and short."

Hidden by banks of fog, the ship bounced through greenish waves. Eveleen leaned against the side, feeling the wind on her face. She listened, with her eyes closed, to the rapid conversation in Modern Greek between Kosta and Stavros coming from belowdecks.

She was glad to be passive for a time. She and Kosta had been forced to spend the night on a little patch of shore, no food, no water, dressed in their wetsuits. Cold had not been the problem, but heat and thirst; they'd resorted to swimming just to get rid of body heat, but of course they couldn't drink the water that surrounded them.

But just after dawn they'd seen the ship emerge from drifting smoke-tinged fog, and by the time they'd swum out, fastened the sled to the underside of the hull, and climbed aboard, Stavros had hot food and coffee waiting.

Finally she heard Kosta's step, and she looked up. He swiped his curly hair back, squinting against the furious glare of the sun, and then he sneezed violently.

"Smoke is worse," he said as Stavros appeared behind him.

Unanswerable. Eveleen just nodded.

"Stav was blown out through the opening to sea during the storm, as we thought. He used the motor to come back in to retrieve us, and stayed close to the cliffs below the main island in order to stay unseen. Very close, or he would not have found it."

Stavros's lips thinned in a smile of triumph, and Eveleen felt her own heart give a jolt.

"So Stavros located a signal?"

"Yes. A strong one, too. It should be almost right underneath the city, along the cliff faces below it."

"We're on our way to investigate now, or ought we to return?"

Kosta turned to Stavros, who rubbed the heels of his hands over his eyes. He'd obviously been up all night, keeping the bow of the ship pointed into the storm so that it wouldn't broach to and sink.

"Let us see now," Stavros said, his accent heavier, his voice raspy. "It is close. The marker might shift if another storm comes."

Kosta grinned. "Get your gear back on," Kosta said, rubbing his hands. "By the time we're ready, Stavo will get us there."

Eveleen set down her empty mug and reached for her mask.

Linnea woke to the sweet sounds of the girls singing.

Another day. It was time for the long purification ritual. All around her, women rose, shook themselves out, and busied themselves with the little tasks, both sacred and homely, that measured out their lives.

I will stay for one more session, Linnea thought. *And then I'll return to Akrotiri and tell them I failed.*

She was thirsty; her stomach growled; her head ached. There seemed to be smoke in the air.

She shut her eyes and turned her attention to the rise and fall of the chanting voices.

On the other side of the great mountain, the Kayu said to Ross and Gordon, "It iss long sstory. I musst breathe. We go?"

Gordon looked Ross's way, leaving the decision to him. Ross remembered the underground cave. It could be that the two Fur Faces had prepared some kind of trap, but why?

No, to get data they were willing to take risks. The particular risk required now was just different than expected.

Ross looked around at the barren rock, the sky full of smoky haze, and just then another tremor rumbled deep underground, sending birds skyward and cascades of small stones clattering down the hillside. Dust rose, hanging suspended in the air.

Ross squinted against the sunlight, watching two swallows fly down into a haze-hidden valley, forked tails streaming after.

"Let's go," he murmured.

Gordon nodded.

The Kayu led the way.

Eveleen dropped below the surface of the water. It was a relief to get her eyes out of the stinging, smoke-laden air.

She looked around, expecting the underwater world to snap into focus, blue and clear. But it, too, was turbid, the lighting a faintly sinister brownish green.

Eveleen looked around past waving fronds and tight schools of tiny fishes running with what seemed to her frantic haste. The fish turned about, flicked, and darted downward at an oblique angle.

She looked up and saw not the sky but a brownish layer. She realized that she'd gotten used to the haze, but it was gradually getting worse.

Kosta tapped her on the shoulder, caught her attention. She turned his way, nodded, and held on as he triggered the sled.

Stavros had been quite firm about the location. He had repeated that the signal was very strong, the device might even be stuck right on the surface of the rock.

Waving sea life indicated turbulent currents; here and there eyes peered out between fronds. The underwater world was so very strange, like another planet, she thought, looking around. Even one's sense of time altered.

But anxiety still remained: that sense of impending disaster, of events about to overtake them. *Get busy and search*, she scolded herself. *Explore later.*

She faced downward, her hand hovering over her forehead, when the sled's steady progress slowed, then stopped. Had he found it already? They both flicked on their lights. And then gazed in surprise.

No device: what they'd found was a great cavern. Kosta swept a hand toward it, an ironic *Shall we?*

In answer Eveleen let go of the sled and swam forward, scanning methodically as she drifted. Kosta joined her; they anchored the sled, and with a few short gestures they divided the territory.

It didn't help that they had no idea what they were looking for. Large? Small? Camouflaged? Out in the open? Eveleen had expected to see something sticking out, some sort of futuristic tech nestled among the weird plants and mossy rocks, right in the open. Stavros had said that the signal was strong, and that meant they had to be right near whatever it was.

But although the variety of rocks, fish, and plants was both rich and amazing, nothing futuristic or tech-made was in sight.

Kosta's entire body was expressive of frustration. He gave one great kick and lunged back to the mouth of the cavern, and then he began feeling over the rock.

Eveleen floated up to the other side and did the same, looking past her bubbles. She had to be careful. There were several kinds of coral, brilliant in color, but sharp and deadly; she did not need a cut in her gloves.

They felt over the rock, and she bent close and examined some of the weirder sea plants. They all looked real enough, but if the aliens were clever enough, she might be fooled. She wasn't any kind of an expert on undersea life, especially in the Mediterranean.

Slowly they worked their way inward, and after a time gave up the tactile exploration. Kosta dove down to sift through the fine sand at the bottom of the cavern. Eveleen kept looking at the vast dark hole. Just how deep was this cave, anyway?

She was strongly tempted to go exploring but forced herself to join Kosta and work over the seafloor.

They'd kicked up quite a bit of sand when Kosta finally sat back, his hands clenched into fists.

Eveleen gestured toward the inner part of the cave. He shrugged: *Why not?* It took him only minutes to cross back to the opening of the cavern and return with the sled.

So they pushed off, relieved to be doing something, at least. Eveleen could feel the coarser hum of the sled's engine, now at its lowest speed.

The lancing blue and yellow sunbeams from the surface very swiftly vanished. They could still see the cave mouth behind them, but light did not penetrate far. Eveleen reached over and turned up the intensity on the sled's headlamp, then turned her own down a bit; her battery power was now reading just above half. She knew there was an emergency supply, but she didn't want to have to rely on that if they had to do another search by feel.

The cave bent suddenly and angled up. Strange. Was the rock smoother?

She turned to Kosta at the same moment he faced her, and pointed. There were no sea plants here, just smooth rock. It was a slab. Could it have been made by a great shifting of land, a quake?

They proceeded at a slow pace, Eveleen watching to her side and Kosta to his, with the sled illumining the way ahead to give maximum visibility.

On and on, and then another sharp turn. The sled banged against the rock as Kosta maneuvered it around.

And then they stopped, staring.

The cave widened; there, settled on the seafloor, rested one of the great globe ships.

Chapter Fifteen

Down in the cave with the machinery, the two Kayu faced the Time Agents. One of them manipulated the computer, or whatever that egg thing was. Ross noted sourly that if his attempt to crash it had been successful, there was no sign of it.

One of the Fur Faces signed something to the other, adding a low comment in its clicking, trilling language, and then from the machine came a voice—in English.

"Our previous study indicates that you respond to this tongue."

Neither man moved.

"We use it in preference to the style of Greek the traders bring here because the vocabulary is easier to adapt to what must be discussed. But first we must reveal to you the fact that we have been waiting for you to appear, that everything is in readiness; it remains for you to make the decision what must occur next."

Who can resist an opening like that?

Ross knew that if he were alone, he'd ride with the wave and see what happened, but he deferred to Ashe, the more senior agent—and the one who made fewer mistakes.

Ashe looked up at Ross, his head canted in question.

If you're asking me, *Ross thought,* I say let's go for it.

Besides, trying to interrogate someone in a language he understood as superficially as he did Ancient Greek was no picnic.

Ashe said, in English, "Proceed."

The Kayu responded with a swift exchange in their own tongue. Though it's usually a mistake to ascribe human emotions to nonhumans, Ross suspected they were excited. And why not? It wasn't just a matter of guessing the right language. These furry guys now had a vector on not just where but when Ross and Ashe had really come from.

"There are devices in place at crucial locations in the volcanic caldera," the machine-translation went on, in a perfectly enunciated, dispassionate tone.

"These devices are not ours but belong to the ****—" The machine failed to translate here, instead giving a name in a humming sort of language. "That is their name for themselves; we call them the !!!."

This time the machine provided some trills and whistles.

Ross, giving in to impulse, said, "If you mean the guys in the blue suits, we call 'em Baldies."

"Baldies." The machine repeated the word in English and then in the clicking tongue, and the two Kayu looked at each other, one of them making asthmatic noises that might have been laughter.

The other touched a control and trilled something.

The machine said, "It is a most appropriate term, for it differentiates between us, does it not?"

A little alien humor there? Ross thought.

He said, feeling weirder by the second, "You definitely aren't bald. And neither am I," he added. "So what's the story on these devices?"

If humor there had been, it was now gone. "They are...even your language does not have the precise concepts, although your physicists could describe them mathematically. Call them...'entropy adjusters,' and you will be close enough."

"Entropy adjusters," Ross repeated, resisting the impulse to wipe his sweaty palms down the sides of his fake-hide skirt.

"Yes," the Kayu stated through the machine. "In effect they transform the energy of the rising magma into a massive gravitational knot rather than allowing it to build up as heat. The effect has been to cool the magma, thus preventing the explosion."

Ross stared, his heart slamming behind his ribs. They were too late? Was the world, now set on a pastoral path of low tech, doomed to Baldy conquest up-time? Then he thought of the found earring...of Eveleen down somewhere in the city...and felt momentary relief, until he realized that if the Baldies managed to change history, Eveleen would never even have existed, and he snapped, "You mean the magma has already cooled off too much?"

"No, there is still time, but we are approaching a point of no return. To complete the process, the devices must discharge the energy harmlessly, in one burst of temporal distortion. That is what brought us here; it is detectable across many centuries."

Something tickled at the back of Ross's mind, but before he could grasp it the other alien trilled something. The first one hesitated.

"My companion would note that this distortion, which affects suitably sensitive minds across a wide span of time, may account for the prevalence of prophecy on your world; I would merely add that this is but one way...you might say *Nemesis*...speaks to sentient beings."

Ross felt momentarily disoriented by the strangeness of the situation. Here he and Ashe were, standing on top of a volcano that was about to blow up with a force that would make a hydrogen bomb look like a mere special effect, and having a metaphysical discussion with aliens.

The alien continued. "The adjusters are still building toward discharge, and if they are destroyed before they complete the discharge, the energy will be released all at once as heat, creating an explosion equivalent to what would have happened without interference."

Ross whistled under his breath—or started to. Remembering the whistling language spoken by the others, he didn't want to inadvertently be saying something he'd get into trouble for.

So the brain boys at home had been right!

Ashe said, "Why have you not acted to destroy these devices? Or don't you know where they are?"

"We know the location of each," one of the Kayu replied. "But we cannot act. It is not our mandate. We have been here, in place, observing, and waiting until you should appear. 'You' being, in this context, someone of your somewhat mysterious people, who appear and then vanish again after violent encounters."

Well, that about sums us up, *Ross thought.*

Ashe said, "So our guesses are correct, then, that if this volcano does not go off, then up the time-line our civilization will not have advanced much past what it is now?"

"This is correct."

"Thus rendering it easier for someone, like the Baldies, say, to take over," Ross stated. He didn't say out loud, but mentally he added: *Or you.*

The second Kayu said, "It is a logical surmise, but it is not correct. The !!!—the Furless Ones, as you would say—are committed to maximizing the biodiversity of the galaxy by protecting aboriginal life-forms."

"Protecting!" Ross's expostulation was almost a snort. "These are the same friendly types who shoot on sight? Don't we count as aboriginal?"

"They protect life, not lives," replied the Kayu. "When they find a space-traveling culture, such as yours is becoming, they locate the original world and search its past for critical points. Then they intervene as necessary to eliminate space flight, so as to contain that life-form and prevent it from contaminating the biosphere of other planets."

"So they are self-constituted galactic ecologists, then?" Ashe asked, brows aslant.

"It is a close enough designation, yes."

Silence.

Ross chewed on that, and Ashe said, "So let's get this straight, then. If we don't mess with their devices, the volcano doesn't blast, things are fine, and we never reach space in our future."

"It is so."

Ross burst out, "But if it hadn't gone off, then we wouldn't exist—and how would you know? For that matter, you said you detected the time explosion, or whatever you would call it, but it hasn't happened yet. And if we decide to destroy the devices, it won't, so how could you detect it?"

The two Kayu held a discussion that intensified into trills, with gestures and quick exchanges. Ross glanced over at Ashe to see him frowning. It was fairly clear that the Kayu, however much they looked alike, did not think alike: one seemed to want to say one thing, and the other something else.

At last one stepped back, permitting the other to address the machine, which stated in its precise English, "This choice you will make creates a major bifurcation in the probability wave that represents your world-line. Two futures so different that it is easy to detect the two states, both of which exist until your decision is carried out. In one, a pastoral planet, little or no EM emissions, the major pollutant being methane from cows; in the other, a technological civilization, heavy EM emissions detectable light years away, with heavy pollution from fossil carbon combustion. Those are but two ways of detecting the two states."

"Schroedinger's cat," said Ashe. "Alive and dead at the same time."

There was a long pause. One of the Kayu did something to the machine, and then both exclaimed softly. Looking up Schroedinger, and his cat? The Kayu trilled, and the machine stated: "Yes, according to your physics texts. You would say, superposition."

"But we've already decided," said Ross. "If we don't stop the explosion, we'll cease to exist—cease to ever have existed. And you still haven't explained how you could detect the time explosion if we prevent it. Or will detect it…"

"There are still courses of action open to the Baldies," replied the Kayu. "Only when these are all eliminated—or carried out—will the waveform collapse and seal your reality. At that point, one way or the other, the result will not be reversible. But all our actions will have been part of that reality, including the detection of the superposition that includes the time explosion. That is always pastward from your decision, and thus always exists."

"My head hurts," muttered Ross.

Perhaps the alien heard him. "Your people have not had time travel long enough to develop the language and concepts to deal with it—although there are hints in various of your… philosophical texts, one might say, and among some cultures, of the proper approach."

"So what do we do? Destroy the machines?"

"No. Not only would that be almost impossible—they are not entirely material—since their mode of operation is time-like, but even if it were, the consequences would be catastrophic. The uncontrolled release of the energy they contain might unravel space-time itself, unmaking your world and all within it."

Ashe let out his breath in a short, not quite silent curse.

I knew I was going to hate this mission, *Ross thought.* Instinct is right every damn time.

Ashe said slowly, "So, might the Baldies do that, if they get desperate enough, just to make sure we never become technological?"

"They would never do such a thing by deliberate action. They value life too highly."

Ross waved a hand. "So you say. But where does the difference between life and lives lie for them? One, ten, a million?"

The Kayu trilled and clicked in what seemed to be distress, and Ashe turned to Ross. "Hold on a moment; let's just go with them for now." He turned to the Kayu. "So these devices. We can just turn them off?"

"No, that would be equally disastrous. But we can introduce chaotic oscillations in the gravitational knot, which will eventually cause the machines to fail. But you must then prevent the Baldies from relinearizing them for at least... seven rotations of the sun, at which point the Baldies cannot use them to abort the volcanic explosion without causing the same type of temporal disaster that destroying them would cause."

"But turning them off will permit the volcano to go off, right?" Ross asked.

"It is so."

Ross thought, There's a time for talk, a time for thought, and a time for action. When they hired me on, it was because I took action. And so far I've been right.

He strolled forward and noted how the Kayu retreated a little. So they were afraid of him. Interesting.

"So where are the controls to these devices?"

"The !!! have the controls proper. We know that they have a ship, but its location is unknown to us." The Kayu indicated the two of them. "There were, when we came to this place in your time-line, two more of us. The others we believe had found their ship, but they are no longer in this life." A trill and some dismal-sounding clicks accompanied this statement, which the Kayu did not have the machine translate.

Ross shook his head. "So my question remains: how many lives?"

The first Kayu said something in their language; the second one spoke into the machine.

"You must understand what their history has been," the machine stated.

"All I need to understand right now is, how do we prevent these—adjusters—from operating?" Ross asked.

One of the slim fur-covered hands touched a thing that looked like a cell-phone with a single button extruded from the computer. "But there is very little time."

Ross didn't understand much about superpositions and gravitational theory, but the concept of time running out was definitely in his ballpark. And the Fur Faces had as much as said it would take seven days for the devices to fail.

He looked at Gordon Ashe, who frowned into the middle distance. Well, it was his job to consider all the angles, to negotiate, to compromise, to find the middle ground.

Ross saw action as his own mandate.

And so he reached forward, and before anyone could say anything more, Ross smacked the cell-phone in the middle of those glowing touch pads.

Its light went out.

"All right, then," Ross said, breathing hard in his sweaty mask. "What's next?"

Chapter Sixteen

When the light shaft reached the gnarled tree-throne, the chanting women brought their ritual to a close, and the seer stepped once again into her seat.

The voices of the girls out on the plateau could be heard rising and falling in pleasing treble tones. This day was almost exactly like the one before; Linnea wondered how the priestesses perceived time, if their experiences blended into an indistinguishable run of days and years.

But she must not be lulled into thinking time did not matter. It did. The smoke burning her eyes and making the back of her throat feel raw was a reminder of that, as were the little tremors that rumbled through the caverns.

Linnea looked up. Was that crack new? Her thoughts scattered when the newest petitioner sat down and spoke in the old language.

Oh, if only Jonathan were here with us, Linnea thought. She could envision the linguist swathed in robes, pretending to be a woman and hiding a recorder so that he could gather precious words to add to the little known about the language still termed Linear A.

The thought of poor Jonathan being a linguistic spy brought a sad sort of smile to Linnea's lips; the reason the agent was not along for this trip was his wife having recently been killed in a car wreck. He was now coping with two small children.

Why couldn't he go ahead in the time machine and then come back?

Or for that matter, could they use the time machine to go back and save her? Linnea wondered, frowning, as the seer began to writhe, her old woman's form taking on the aspect of the holy serpent. What would it harm? What would it change, besides making a family whole and happy again? Could such an action unravel the world's proper course? What, given the horrors of history, constituted "proper"?

"Assssssssah!"

The seer's hiss turned into a long, gargled shout, her eyes wide and blind.

Everyone stopped, eyes turned toward the seer.

Her hands snaked out, waving. In that strange, hoarse, wailing cry she shouted words, repeating some phrases over and over.

The priestesses looked at one another in bewilderment and in fear. Then the oldest one motioned to the others. "Get the girls. Go down the mountain now. Tell everyone that the goddess has spoken at last: the people, all people, are to live now on the blue water, under the blue sky. Now, at once, before the sun sleeps."

The younger priestesses vanished through the crevasse leading to the plateau.

Linnea lingered, puzzled, confused. Another tremor shook the mountain, a gentle one, but a cascade of little stones poured down through the skylight crack, some of them falling on her.

"Go," Ela urged, touching Linnea's arm. "The goddess has spoken to us all. You must go; everyone must go. The fire spirits have been released, and their battle with the earth is to begin. There will be safety only on the water, in the air, away from rock and earth and fire."

What did that mean?

Linnea knew one thing for certain: she must find the rest of her team.

She bundled up her skirts into her arms and scooted between the rock slabs, her awareness of their weight, of the inexorable press of stone against stone and how it could so easily crush her, driving her headlong in urgency—and fear.

Thit thing isn't old, Eveleen thought, looking at the globe ship.

At first she'd assumed it was another find, perhaps a crashed ship from farther back in prehistory. But as she flippered closer, examining the smooth glasslike substance that formed the hull, she realized that there were no barnacles on it, no sea life attached. If the material was somehow impervious to the amazing adaptability of sea life, it would be a first.

No, this thing is new, or at least, it's newly here.

It's the Baldy ship, she thought then, looking at it in amazement.

Just then a puff of dust caught her eye and she turned her head. The sea life glowing along the cavern walls waved wildly, and rocks tumbled with hypnotizing slowness through the water.

Quake! Another of those little ones.

She turned her attention to Kosta, who waved an arm at the ship.

She looked down. Before, it had been difficult to make out anything, but now, suddenly, the interior of the ship lit with a variety of colors, some of them blinking quickly. Alarms?

What it meant was, someone might just be along to deal with it. Someone with weapons.

A touch on her arm made her recoil. Eveleen realized her heartbeat was up, adrenaline racing through her system. Danger! Only where?

Kosta pointed upward. Eveleen looked, and where there had been darkness before, a smooth cylindrical vertical shaft, made of clear glass, touched down to the top of the globe ship. She had missed it before; they both flippered up and felt it, solid, smooth, airtight.

Kosta pointed down into the ship. Around the equator, lights chased, the same blue-white cold light of the transporter mechanisms.

Kosta jerked his head toward the ship, and inside his mask, she saw him grin. It was his pirate grin, and she gasped, realizing what he wanted to do: steal the globe ship!

Why not?

Both of them now turned their attention to the ship. How to get into it without it flooding?

But Kosta had learned something about the alien tech. He sped upward again, feeling along the outer connection between the tube shaft and the globe ship. She saw him straighten out, manipulating something.

Clank! Whirr! Sounds reverberated, weirdly flattened, through the water: under the shaft something slid shut in the ship, and then the tube retracted a foot or so.

Kosta then motioned to Eveleen. He mimed pushing the ship, waved his hand at the sled. *Pushing?*

Well, why not? It wasn't one of the huge deep-space twelve-crew jobs, like the one that had taken them to the faraway library planet, last mission. This one was small, everything right there: a two – or four-seater scout craft, she'd call it. And under water, it was just mass they had to deal with, which merely took patience.

Kosta ran the sled up to within a few feet of the side of the ship and let it sink slowly while he reached into a pouch and pulled out a brick of some plastic material. He began to mold it into a pancake, then slapped it on the nose of the sled and revved its engine to ram it gently into the ship. He began to pulse the engine, slowly. At first the mass resisted: it was as though nothing was happening. But eventually, the globe began to rock ever so slightly, and then more and more as he timed the engine pulses carefully. Finally, with a puff of mud squirting from underneath, the ship moved up into the water!

Then began a strange ultra-slow-motion bat-and-ball game, with the biggest ball Eveleen had ever seen. They maneuvered the globe ship through the cavern, back to the access tunnel.

Getting out was a lot faster than coming in, now that they didn't have to explore every inch of the walls. They sped as fast as they could, pushing the globe ship faster and faster until it finally shot out of the cavern into the water and dropped slowly down to the seafloor below.

What now? A little beeping noise warned her that *now* was the right time to get to the surface: she was on her emergency air.

Kosta pointed upward. Ah, there was the ship.

As Eveleen grabbed hold of the sled she caught sight of the alien-tech device, and saw that it had gone blank. Batteries? Broken?

They refastened the sled to the ship and surfaced. Her mind was full of questions. Beside her, Kosta shoved back his mask and looked up at Stavros.

"We found one of their ships. Moved it to the seafloor below," he gasped.

Stavros was already reaching over the side to hand them up. "I will put a marker down. But something happened here: the target went dead," he said.

They looked at his alien tech-location device. It was just as blank as the one Kosta had carried.

Rumbling from the cliffs not four hundred yards away brought all three of them around. Strange little waves propagated out and high up a section of cliff gave way, causing a landslide. They watched the slab of rock smash into the water, sending seaweed-veined water shooting up.

When the sound had diminished, Kosta said, "Something has happened. We must get back."

Stavros did not wait for an answer—not that Kosta or Eveleen would have argued.

More tremors shook the cliffs as the ship moved back toward the harbor area. Eveleen, looking up at Akrotiri built into the cliffs overhead, like steps, made mental calculations and looked back again.

That underwater cave, the one that had connected the shaft with the globe ship. Could that perhaps lead up to that mysterious little room high up on the edge of the city?

Another question, she thought grimly, but before she could say anything, Kosta exclaimed, "Look!"

Stavros exclaimed something in idiomatic Greek.

They all turned their attention westward. Streams of people moved down the road at a frantic pace, many of them carrying bulky objects on their backs. Eveleen, squinting against the glaring sunlight, counted at least three looms, several rolled rugs, and uncountable jars and reed-mat bundled objects.

"It's an evacuation," she said.

Stavros thumped a fist onto the rail. "We must find Ashe."

And Ross, Eveleen said, but silently.

"We must first defend the boat," Kosta stated with grim portent. "If this is the big evacuation that the scientists posited, in reality that means people are going to do anything, anything at all, to get themselves a ship."

Chapter Seventeen

Linnea heard women's voices behind her and halted on the trail. A cluster of older women appeared, huddling around something. Two of them looked up in mute appeal, and Linnea hurried back up the trail to discover that the three women had fashioned a kind of stretcher from two staffs lashed together with lengths of woven fibers of some sort and cloth laid over the whole. On this stretcher lay the seer, her face blanched.

"She cannot walk," Ela gasped. "The goddess departed from her spirit with such speed, she could not at first find her body."

Meaning, she got herself a migraine? Linnea thought, reaching for the end of one of the staffs. Ela paused to tuck the linen shroud more securely around the poor woman; then she picked up her end and they started down the trail.

At first they tried to keep their steps in sync, but the trail narrowed so abruptly in places it became nearly impossible. Added to that was the frustration of stumbling and slipping over stones that one could not see.

Before too long Linnea's hands ached, and her clothing was damp with sweat. *At least I get some exercise*, she thought with bleak humor; how the other women managed, she did not know. But her mind raced on, and she watched it race, amazed at how one's thoughts will catch at any diversion from threatening danger: as a long tremor, one with a sickening jolt in the middle of it, silenced and stilled them all, what flitted through her stream of consciousness was the absurdity of discussing exercise machines with women who had lived three thousand years before she was born.

When the tremor stopped, they picked up their poles and started forward, halting again when an ominous rattling above heralded a landslide.

Hastening back up the trail, they watched in fear as boulders leaped crazily down, one smashing onto the trail and sending a chunk of it scattering down the hillside below. A hail of rubble followed, ending at last with a pall of choking dust.

"Come. We must push through," Ela cried hoarsely.

They stepped gingerly over the layer of dirt and stones nearly obliterating the trail and hurried on.

Abruptly the trail widened, and they were able to establish a rhythm. If the seer disliked the swinging, jolting stretcher, she said nothing; she gripped the poles at each side, her eyes closed.

The sun began to sink toward the west, and thirst had gone from pestering to agonizing when Linnea realized dully that they were rounding the last hill.

A gasp from Ela brought the stretcher parade to a halt. Her face, weirdly lit, was turned toward the north. Linnea stared in fear and wonder at the pre-Kameni Island, or what she assumed was that island.

The land itself was utterly obscured by a sky-scraping black cloud, one that had to be reaching at least twenty miles into the air. The cloud was not solid: writhing columns of smoke, from which flames of fire darted, reached like the fingers of death into the east.

"The holy snakes," one of the women whispered, in awe.

Without any warning at all the women were flung against the cliff side and then down onto the ground.

Pain lanced through Linnea's shoulder, but she was only peripherally aware of it. Why was the world sideways?

"Ayah," a voice moaned.

Linnea felt something sting her cheek, and who was pushing her so hard?

The ground, air, and sky roared, jolting her so forcefully she could not struggle to her elbows. Tiny stones clattered all around, pinging her face and arms as she tried to see who was moaning. Black surged overhead, darting down flames toward the mountain from which they had just come.

Clack! Something dark flickered across her vision; there was a pain across her temple, and the world went dark.

"What the—" Stavros never finished his exclamation.

As the three watched, the island seemed to shrug, and then shudders rippled down in rings from the mountain, churning the water into nervous, choppy wavelets.

They had come to a halt maybe a quarter mile from the shoreline, to avoid trouble. From there they watched the swarms of people pouring into every imaginable type of vessel, from the beautifully painted and decorated pleasure boats to the single-masted tradecraft.

As one boat veered near, Stavros shouted in Ancient Greek, "Where does everyone go?"

"The seer has spoken! The goddess says to live on the water, under the sky! The earth and fire demons are going to battle! I go to warn the other towns!" He pulled on the rope controlling his sail, and the little boat glided away toward the pre-Kameni Island.

Stavros turned to the other two, who shrugged. What the heck did that mean, other than "get out of here"? Had the Baldies somehow manipulated the oracle?

Whatever had happened, the entire population of Akrotiri appeared to have taken seriously the command to evacuate.

Even fishing smacks and little rowboats were crowded so dangerously some of them were so low the rails were a hand's breadth above water.

Eveleen watched as the evacuation began in an orderly fashion, turning desperate on the edges: there were, as Kosta had predicted, some fights for some of the boats. She winced, wishing there was something she could do, but they were helpless to interfere.

She watched one small family, consisting of a woman and two children, shoved back away from a skinny little fishing smack. The woman ran, crying, from one boat to another, until at last one of the great, decorated boats of the priests paused, and she and her children were pulled on.

That was when the side of the mountain gave a heave, and quake waves fled outward, flinging people down onto the ground, sending donkeys braying, goats scolding, and every bird on the island winging into the air, squawking in angry protest.

"It's the big quake," Eveleen whispered, appalled, but afraid to look away.

Wave after wave of shaking toppled walls, and cracks spiderwebbed up the few standing higher buildings. Then, with majestic slowness, the three-story buildings came crashing down, walls crumbling in either direction.

From somewhere jugs emerged, rolling down a cliff, some smashing, others hopping, until they fell a hundred yards into the sea below. Flames shot up somewhere else, as up in the sky, great writhing clouds of black sent out deadly jets of burning flame to lick the top of the mountain.

"Oil," Kosta said, pointing.

All it would take was one untended lamp and spilled olive oil; the flames spilled hungrily from the windows of a storehouse, just to be doused by the thunderous rumble and choking dust of a landslide.

On and on the shaking went, the clouds moving eastward raining down black bits of obsidian first in boulders, then in rocks, then pebbles, and finally in small, stinging bits of glass, until at last the firestorm and motion gradually subsided. By now the waves shuddered back and forth, some slapping back up onto the beaches, drenching terrified people, forcing them back up onto land.

But down they came again, from wherever they had been hiding during the deluge of burning rock, carrying children, animals, birds, and household goods, to cram into the boats.

Eveleen turned her head. Already many of the ships and boats were plying southward as fast as they could, oars rising and falling with fear-driven jerks, sails tautened by terror-strengthened hands.

They would get away. Maybe they would even make it to Crete, their beautifully painted jugs and vases to influence the painters there into a new style, a new way of looking at the world.

Eveleen, with a mental shrug, wished them well, and turned her attention back to the shoreline.

Where was Ross?

"Let us land," Stavros said at last. "Over there, out of sight of the evacuation. We must find Murdock, Ashe and Linnea Edel."

Chapter Eighteen

After Ross's "What's next?" he stepped back to wait for a reaction.

Ashe shook his head, but before he could speak, the Kayu spoke with clear urgency into the translator.

"This segment of the mountain is unstable. We will have to evacuate at once. The onset of chaos in the gravitational knot is releasing more energy than we expected. Now the Earth must find its balance point again."

Action, reaction.

Ashe said grimly, "It's going to be interesting, getting down the mountain if he means what I think he means."

Ross and Gordon turned their attention to the aliens, who had embarked on a fast exchange.

Gordon muttered under his breath, "I wish I could reverse that damn translator of theirs."

Then the first Kayu beckoned to the two Time Agents. "We shall give you our two wind vessels, though you cannot use our *** for returning to the mountain. But you do not need that."

Wind vessels? Ross mouthed the words to Ashe.

Ashe said under his breath, "Use 'em to spy on the Greeks and Baldies, I'll bet."

"You musst come now," the Kayu said.

Ross and Ashe followed the swaying robes, not back to the surface, but farther inside. Ross noted that they passed the room where he and Eveleen had been imprisoned for a night, and then they were all three enclosed in a cylindrical elevator shaft made of some stonelike white material, with a source of light impossible to detect.

A whoosh of air carrying a faint smell of ozone hit their faces, but they felt no accompanying drop in stomach like one experienced with elevators in their own time. Ross didn't know if they'd gone up, down, or sideways. The opaque door slid open again, and they emerged onto a cliff. Hot, smoky wind teased hair and clothing; the smell of sulfur fingered its way in even past their breathing masks.

The Kayu touched some kind of control that Ross didn't see because of the limited field of vision caused by his mask; a section of what had looked like solid rock flickered out of existence, leaving what at first appeared to be two giant bird shapes.

"Hang gliders," Ashe said.

"Sort of," Ross amended. He'd been hang gliding with Eveleen. These things looked different.

The Kayu said in its hissing speech, "It holdss humanss."

Gordon gave a shrug and bent over the closest one. Ross also bent, but what he tried to spot was the video projector that had projected the holographic rock. He couldn't find anything, even when he ran his hands over the rough pumice.

"Come on," Gordon said.

A tremor growling deep underground underscored the urgency.

He and Ross dragged the gliders out. At once the wind tried to take them, even though the wings were folded down.

Gordon examined them swiftly; from the look on his face he was doing some fast mental calculations.

Ross bent his attention to the controls, which appeared to be simple. Levers controlled the wing struts and the tails: levers for hands up front, for feet at the back. Out beyond the glider platform someone had painted great glassy bird-eyes on either side of a raptor's beak. So the Kayu had used these to glide in the air over the island, then, and to the locals they would look like giant birds. Had the Baldies seen them? If they were just gliding, there would be no energy signature to detect.

His thoughts were broken when Gordon thumped his arm and pointed. "Lie here. Strap in like this. I think we'll need to balance them for weight up front," Gordon said. "I suspect, from the look of these things, that the Kayu are lighter than we are."

"Is this a really stupid idea?" Ross asked Gordon as they dragged the gliders to the back of the cliff, giving themselves maximum running room. The straps, Ross noted, were made from some silky material that had enormous tensile strength. "I mean, where did that Fur Face go?"

"I don't know, but it looks as if this is the only way down," Gordon said. "And if they've used them, well, so can we." His mouth tightened in an ironic smile.

Another tremor shook the mountain, this one with an odd, jolting hop in it. A sudden roar beneath them sent both men to the edge of the cliff. Far down, just barely visible in the haze, they saw a tremendous landslide.

"Right," Ross said. "Let's get out of here."

"Now or never," Gordon agreed.

They gripped the handles of the gliders, flicked up the wings, and began to run.

Almost at once the gliders bucked and sidled as the wings and the wind played tug-of-war. Five, four, three, two—

There was the cliff edge, with a thousand-foot drop beyond. Ross's palms prickled with sweat, his heart thumped in his ears, as he swung himself out and slammed onto the platform.

The straps slapped themselves round him, the nose edged over the cliff, and the glider dropped.

"Whoo-*eeeeeee*!" The sound tore out of Ross as his guts plummeted, then the wind current caught the glider and tossed it up back toward the cliff.

"Bank! Bank!" Gordon roared from fifty feet away and out.

Ross turned his head, saw the cliff zooming toward him. He jammed his feet against the tail controls and the right wing; the glider banked sharply, sailing with amazing smoothness within a yard of the rocky face of the cliff, then outward and away.

There below was the entire island ring, visible between gouts of smoke rising to join the sheep-backed clouds flocking eastward from the south. *Storm coming*, Ross thought as he lifted his head and gazed to the north. There, beyond the north shore of Akrotiri's peninsula, were the green waters surrounding the pre-Kameni Island. Weird whitish water spoiled the emerald perfection of that vast lagoon. Steam vents?

Not a storm, Ross thought in slow, chilling shock as his wing moved and he could see past it to the huge, black, tentacled plume thrusting up from the island. It was not a storm, but something far worse: an eruption from what would very soon—maybe even now—be the center of the entire caldera.

Are we too late?

That question, too, was swept away when the quake hit.

Afterward, Ross could never pinpoint where the fault slipped. What he became aware of first was the sound, a great, roaring, grinding growl deeper and more terrifying than mere thunder, which was just air. This sound was far more powerful, the restless shifting of immeasurable strata as magma began forcing its way upward. What Ross saw were rings chasing outward, and then reverberating back, through both land and water.

The gliders emerged round a great fold in the mountain just in time for Ross and Gordon to look down and see Akrotiri trembling, like a toy city when children stomp on the floor all around. With excruciating slowness the remaining roofs toppled inward as walls fell outward, sending rubble, broken furnishings and jars, and clouds and clouds of reddish gold dust spewing into the air.

"Up," Gordon shouted. "Under the cliff, as close as you can!"

Ross didn't need the order. He already had his wings spread to the maximum, riding the updraft. Overhead the snaking tunnels of fire-laden smoke reached out, burning everything they touched. The two Time Agents would be barbecued in midair unless they used the quaking mountain as protection.

A terrifying rain of black stone smashed down behind Ross into the sea, sending up hissing steam columns, some of them high enough to mix in with the smoke overhead.

Hot air whooshed round the cliffs, followed by cold drafts. Both men fought to keep their craft within the lee of relative protection. It was the hot steamy drafts that kept them airborne. They circled round and round, the wings sometimes rattling and trembling as occasional shots of fine glassy black rock rained over them and then fell to the sea below, until, at last, the worst of the fiery smoke began to subside.

They could not stay up forever; already they were circling lower and lower.

It was time to try to land. They did not want to fall on the still-shaking ground anywhere near that city, or on the slipping cliffs that slid down here and there on the mountainsides.

They arced away from their cliff shelter and flew out over the ocean, both looking back, trying to see past the great stretches of their wings.

"What's that?" Gordon cried, peering down through the drifting smoke.

They had emerged far enough around the goat-tracked cliffs to see the harbor, which was filled with little craft, most of them with handkerchief-size sails luffing in the wind.

"Evacuation, looks like!"

"Our people must have found something out," Gordon shouted back.

Ross frowned, looking down there. *Eveleen, where are you?* he called silently.

Now they were out beyond the city, which mostly lay in ruins. Not all the buildings had fallen, but most. They did not see any bodies on those rubble-filled narrow streets. Still, Ross felt his guts tighten. Just because they couldn't see past all the rubble and the smoke didn't mean things weren't really bad.

A fretful gust of wind shook the glider, making the wings clatter, and the nose dove down. Ross tightened his grip on the controls and managed to get the craft to straighten out.

Ross stilled the trembling in his fingers, renewed his grip on the handholds, and urged the glider upward again, trying to gain altitude and time. He glanced over. Gordon was about twenty feet above him, maybe fifty feet away. Ross could see Gordon squinting through the smoke and dust haze to the shores.

Ross turned his attention downward. Would they see Baldies even if they were there? He remembered the business about holographic images. Both the Baldies and the Kayu had them. They definitely had the tech edge; the Time Agents hadn't even dared use their radios.

That would have to change, Ross thought. Meanwhile, what's to keep them from shooting at us up here?

Yet they drifted on, and nothing happened. As they emerged from one dust cloud, they could see the crumbled remains of tiny villages dotting the lower peninsula of the crescent-shaped island. I *hope the people got out,* Ross thought.

Reminded of the evacuation, Ross craned his neck and looked directly below. They were nearly past the harbor now. On the shore chaotic scrambling resolved into some desperate fights to gain ships: as he watched a line of men emerged from one of the rocky hills behind the farthest warehouses and ran down to the shore, where they attacked a family trying to load household items onto a fishing boat. Ross watched in growing but impotent anger as the burly men struck down family members; his fists tightened unconsciously on the controls, momentarily sending his glider bucketing dangerously in the wind. He shifted his attention to fighting for stability, and when the craft had smoothed out, though the wings hummed and rattled, he looked back. He was relieved to see that two parties of fisher folk had come to the aid of the family. Ross's last glimpse of the altercation was of the attackers, now tiny dots, retreating into the hills.

The hills. He frowned, thinking—

"There's our ship," Gordon shouted.

Ross whipped his head around and saw Gordon pointing downward. Well beyond the mass of boats drifting south lay their own craft. As Ross stared into the sunlight, he thought he caught a brief glint from field glasses.

"Let's aim for 'em," he called, pointing with his chin."After you," Gordon answered.

Ross banked his glider. Now that the flight was nearly over, he discovered he was almost sorry.

He realized they were going to have to crash-land on the water and wondered if the gliders would survive. He wondered if he would survive.

The air currents buffeted them hard, cold, hot, sulfur-and-hot-rock-smelling, dust-laden, cold again. Their speed increased as they spiraled downward. The horizon tipped up crazily; for a moment all Ross could see was dark green.

Then the ship revolved into view, passing again. Ross caught a glimpse of Eveleen's pale face. She stood on the taffrail, poised to dive.

Down, and he spread the wings in a desperate attempt to flatten out. Splash! That was Gordon, hitting the water.

Ross skimmed just above the waves. White water splashed up, making him gasp. Then he hit, and would have been wrenched badly had the straps not retracted with efficient, alien speed. He rolled off the platform and plunged into water.

After that nearly effortless flight, he felt heavy, clumsy. He splashed, kicking up his feet, and then struck out swimming.

A moment later an arm appeared, and there was Eveleen. Hands closed around his neck, and lips met his, warm/cold, in a trembling, salty kiss.

Chapter Nineteen

"All right," Gordon Ashe said at last. "What have we got?"

Eveleen scooted closer to Ross. She was not the least bit cold—if anything, the air was more sultry than it had been during the day—but the amount of EM in the air, left over from the extraordinary fire the day before and the lightning now, and the subsonic rumblings that came ever more frequently, put her flight-or-fight instincts on overdrive.

Rain hammered down on the canopy overhead, a drenching, stinging rain full of grit and dust. The fleet had vanished southward during a fierce, blood-crimson sunset, the last sails tiny dots on the horizon as the limb of the sun vanished in a sinister purple haze.

For a time the outriding storm clouds had paraded on to the east, underlit like a villain's face in an old movie. There was nothing subtle in that spectacular sunset; the colors were brilliant, as if the sky had been painted by all the ancient gods with their elemental passions.

Lightning flaring from time to time promised no mercy during the night, either; before they'd exchanged stories, Ashe and Stavros both insisted everyone get the ship battened down.

Because of that quake the island was no longer safe at night, not without a thorough exploration. One thing for certain about major quakes: you never get just one. There are always aftershocks, and some of these can be as bad as the original event.

So they'd all worked to get equipment locked down, and Stavros had used the engines to move the ship eastward to a little cove that might afford some protection from the oncoming weather. There was no one around to hear the growl of the engines, not with the continuous rumble of thunder across the sky.

While Stavros had directed the battening down, Kosta had fired up the microwave and brought out some frozen food from the emergency rations cache. They all had earned a good meal, and it was quite unlikely they would be able to forage on the island anymore. As they ate, each took turns talking about their experiences since the last time they'd met—a time that seemed to Eveleen at least a week ago.

Now they sat crowded on the half-deck below the canopy, Eveleen and Ross together on a hammock, the Greeks perched on barrels that masked advanced tech, and Gordon Ashe on the only fold-down chair.

"What have we got?" Ashe asked again, looking around at the four faces.

Eveleen sipped gratefully from her mug of hot coffee and said, "Nobody saw Linnea, so she's still missing."

"And we will make searching for her top priority," Ashe responded. "Next?"

Ross said, "If we can believe the Kayu, we have a week to make certain the entropy device is not reversed. The Baldies have to know that."

"And will be acting accordingly. We'll get back to them," Ashe said.

"Do you believe the Kayu?" Eveleen asked.

"Yes, I believe them. At least, I can perceive no benefit to be gained from their going to all the trouble to contact us just to lie."

The others nodded, looking tired and strained.

"So we will say we have seven days to keep the Baldies busy. After that, the blow could happen anytime; both sides will be scrambling to leave."

Eveleen winced, thinking of the many threats implied in his flat statement.

"We have the globe ship," Kosta said.

"A globe ship," said Ross. "Could be there were only two Baldies and the rest holos, or maybe there's another?"

"There's rarely been more than one in any other encounter, has there? I mean with Baldies real-time?" asked Eveleen. "If I remember right, the science team decided they were spread really thin; otherwise, with their tech advantages, they'd have taken over long ago."

"If you believe the Kayu, the Baldies aren't interested in conquest, just stopping space flight. But I still believe they are indeed spread thin, so I'm betting your undersea globe ship is the only one in this time/space. So here are our three main areas of action, as I see it," Ashe said, holding up his hand. "We have to keep the globe ship out of the Baldies' hands to prevent them from damping the oscillations and again shunting off the energy building up to the big blow."

"We're going to have to stay out of their mitts," Ross said. "That won't be easy. They have the seek-and-find tech, and what little we've got is easy for them to detect."

"And we're alone on the island now, or nearly," Eveleen said. "And I'm including Linnea. The Kallistans have evacuated, as the archaeologists predicted. That leaves just us and the Baldies—"

"And the Kayu," Ashe put in.

"Right," she said. "And the Kayu. But the Baldies are the ones who are going to know that anything that moves and isn't them is a target."

Ross shook his head. "I still wonder about that 'they value life' talk that the Kayu tried to hand us."

Eveleen said, "Perhaps the Baldies warned the oracle. After all, someone had to, or how did they know to get the people out?"

Ross shrugged. "Gordon and I were with the Kayu, so they certainly didn't. But maybe one or the other of them had some way of warning those priestesses." He frowned, then recalled his flight down. "At any rate, there's one more gang out there, unless they did manage to get the boat. Out from the brush behind the warehouses came a slew of guys…" He went on to describe the attack on the fishing boat.

Eveleen rubbed her forehead. "Wait a minute. Behind the warehouse?"

"Yes," Ross said. "I was just wondering whether these might have been responsible for the attack on our camp, and not the Baldies, when we first landed."

"We will have to keep these men in mind, but there is nothing to be done about them now." Ashe sat back, cradling his coffee in his hands. "To return to our first dilemma, it makes sense that either or both sets of aliens had that cave wired. If they were studying the Kallistans at all, it seems to me that the first place you'd go is where all of them go, to their oracle. Listening to what went on there must have given them the local languages, at least, and clues to customs as well."

Eveleen snapped her fingers. "So their egg-computer has what Linnea wanted so badly: a full dictionary of words corresponding to Linear A!"

Ross nodded once. "Ah. And what can be wired for sound can go both ways. Maybe they broadcast 'voices' for the Kallistan priestesses to hear."

"Well, if the Baldies tried to save the Kallistans, and I hope they did, why have they shot at us in the past?" Eveleen asked.

"Well, if they're hyperecologists of some sort, as the Kayu said, maybe they think of it as pruning," Ashe replied, finishing off his coffee. "We're spinning out in guesswork. Too much of that without facts is just a waste of time. I suggest we all get some shut-eye while we can. At least this storm ought to mask searches, giving us some time for rest. As soon as it's light, you two had better secure that globe ship." He nodded at the Greek agents. "Once we have it, we can explore it on our time, and maybe figure out a way to permanently disable their entropy adjusters."

Kosta grunted in agreement and tossed the dregs of his coffee overboard.

They all settled down then. Eveleen realized her head ached. Trying to keep quiet she reached into the pouch she wore under her flaring skirt, pulled out some sinus tabs.

Now what? The prospect of trying to swallow them in a dry mouth made her stomach churn.

Lightning flared, a vivid purple slash across the sky. She saw a hand reach toward her from one of the other hammocks, holding out a cup of purified water. In grateful silence she took it, swallowed the tabs. Thunder banged and crashed, dying away in a ragged grumble; she heard someone else popping tabs from a seal-pac.

She passed the cup on, felt fingers take it.

Then she lay back down, and despite the storm doing its best to battle the volcano for mastery of sky, earth, and water, she fell deeply asleep.

Just about the time Eveleen fell asleep, Linnea woke up, gasping. Rain slashed down out of the sky, a pitiless downpour. By the flare of lightning Linnea saw that all the priestesses were now awake, two of them bending over a third.

What could they do? Where could they go? At least the air was not cold. They would not freeze. But as a fairly severe aftershock rumbled below the ground, louder than the thunder, Linnea worried about landslides. Mudslides, caused by those frightening steam vents.

A hot, sharp smell brought her head around. Fire, the most ancient threat of all, made her scrabble back in the mud. Moments later vague shapes appeared. Lightning flared again, and then lights snapped into being. Linnea blinked, dazzled.

"Come. Rise and come this way." The voice was tenor, flat, the accent in the Ancient Greek impossible to guess at.

The lights shifted to a trail that steamed, despite the pouring rain. *Am I hallucinating?* Linnea thought.

"Ah!" A woman's voice gave a soft cry of anguish, and Linnea turned again.

The lights snapped over to the priestesses, revealing Ela and one other holding up the older woman who Linnea had decided was second in command to the seer. The seer herself was on her feet, her clothing sodden with mud. She looked old and frail and very unhappy.

"Her arm," Ela said in a frightened voice. "She fell, and hurt her arm, when the ground shook."

"She must walk," came one of those flat tenor voices.

That's not Ross, or Stavros, or Kosta, and it certainly isn't Gordon, *Linnea thought. She said in tentative Ancient Greek,* "Who is it?"

The figures remained behind the lights, perceptible as no more than shadows. Lightning flared again, but Linnea had been looking at the ground. She turned her head, too late.

Thunder crashed right overhead, making her teeth ache. Another lightning bolt illuminated the scene. Linnea watched the ground again, the abnormally flat ground: someone, she realized, had cleared a new path. But the ground was smoking. Was it some freak of the volcano? No, the edges were straight, as though a beam of heat had cut through the rock and soil.

She stepped tentatively forward onto the steaming soil. The soles of her sandals did not burn, so she led the way, the priestesses coming slowly behind. Behind them were the rescuers, shining their lights ahead, down the path that they had made.

For a long time they walked, as the warm, dust-laden acid rain washed the mud from their clothing, stinging their eyes.

The world revolved gently, and Linnea staggered once or twice, trying to breathe deeply against the dizziness. The playing lights, the rain thrumming against nose and mouth, didn't help. Every time the poor woman behind her gasped in pain, Linnea's insides tightened.

Crazy hopes ran through her mind. Were their rescuers perhaps from the Project? Maybe the Project of the future? Linnea couldn't recall anyone talking about weapons that burned away landslides, creating a flat pathway. But she was sure they hadn't told her anything they didn't think she needed to know.

Only now she did need to know.

On and on.

The entire trip was conducted in silence, until at last a cliff loomed, blacker than the surrounding night. One moment rain pattered, loud, in their ears, and then it withdrew into a hissing curtain behind them, and Linnea could breathe. She realized that they had entered a cave of some sort. Faint bluish light glowed at one end, through a rough archway.

A hand touched the back of her shoulder, urging her toward their light. She obeyed the unspoken command, and was glad to do so. Light, shelter, maybe food? Oh, and clean, dry clothing?

But… what about these women? Linnea thought, her expectations withering away. The Project would surely not permit anyone to see modern technical gear, electric lights, and machine-stitched towels and clothes?

Through another archway, into a round room that was again lit by bluish light. Linnea had just enough time to see that there was nothing in it but shapeless cloth of some sort on the floor, and then she turned around as the others entered.

The last priestess walked in, and Ela and the others eased the wounded woman down. Linnea ignored them, trying to empty her mind, staring at the two figures in the doorway: two figures who were slim, of medium height, their fine features quite hairless, their clothing a shimmery suit of bluish purple.

Baldies.

They had not been rescued; they had been captured, by the Baldies.

Then a door slid soundlessly shut, locking them in. She released her breath; they hadn't singled her out. She remembered the warnings about those blue suits and telepathy. Perhaps the fear of the women around her had masked her own thoughts; perhaps their suits couldn't distinguish thoughts in people close together, especially when all of them had to be radiating fear quite powerfully.

"Where are we?" someone asked softly.

"I do not recognize this place," the seer replied, her voice tremulous. "I very much fear that our own house might have fallen in the shaking."

Linnea hesitated, unsure about speaking. What could she say?

Chapter Twenty

"I think," Ashe said, "we'll just have to assume that the Kayu are either dead or in hiding. There is no way to get back up that mountain to the cave where we met them, and even if we did, what would we do or say?"

"We might get them to explain how they think the Baldies are respectful of life," Ross muttered.

Ashe's mouth twitched. "You just can't leave that alone, can you? I admit that the same question has crossed my mind as well. But we'll have to leave that one for leisure moments. Right now, let's go down today's checklist."

It was morning, the full glare of morning. Steam rose from shingle on the beach and from the ruins of Akrotiri, drying in the sunlight half a mile away. They had been shaken awake by a quake sharp enough to rock the boat.

Still, they had landed directly below the ruins of the city. There was no human sound beyond what they made; the harbor, so busy the day before, was empty, the only life the cawing seabirds overhead. Farther up the mountain, swallows darted and chased, their tails streaming.

Ross clipped his radio to the outside of his belt. Now that the need for disguise was over, he wore baggy work pants with sturdy pockets. Eveleen and Stavros stood there in diving gear, Stav with a foot propped on the taffrail. Kosta had changed to a rough linen work shirt and baggy pants.

"Do we all understand the codes?" Ashe went on, tapping his radio.

"Understood," Kosta stated.

"Got it," Ross said.

Eveleen nodded once, biting her lip. Behind her, Stavros half-raised a hand in agreement.

Ashe looked around. "We transmit only when we have to, and we transmit only the codes, and only on the move. If we discover we need to refine the codes, they can wait until tomorrow. Got it?"

Again a round of nods.

"All right, then. Stavros, will you issue the weapons?"

In silence Stavros removed three modified energy weapons from the locker below. These weapons were the reason Eveleen was on the diving team and not on the search team. She would defend herself with the expertise of the martial artist, but she was not certain she could bring herself to use one of these energy weapons and had said so up front.

Ashe turned to her now. "You two know what to do, right?"

"Get the globe ship into a hidden cove, camouflage it, and if we have time, try to get inside."

"Good. Just be back here by sunset, so we can gather with no lights showing. If this place becomes unsafe, we'll let one another know," Ashe repeated, looking from one to another.

Again they nodded, and that was it. Ashe and Ross maneuvered the smaller rowboat out and splashed it into the water. Then they and Kosta climbed over, Ross settling into the stern, the others sitting side by side and manning the oars as Ross kept lookout.

No one spoke. Ross sent a private glance at his wife, to catch a smile in return and a tiny wave of her hand. Then she turned away, reaching for her scuba gear. Stav said something to her in a voice too low for him to hear.

Ross shifted his gaze to the coastline stretching away to the west. It was quite a sight: the shore was lined with an unappetizing tangle of sea brack and dead fish. Unappetizing to humans, at least. An astonishing variety of birds dove and cried and cawed, each flap or peck sending up dark clouds of flies. The smell of sulfur, brine, and rotting fish made Ross breathe through his mouth.

Ashe and Kosta rowed swiftly. Ross kept scanning the coast, not just for slim hairless figures but for suspicious blurs: over breakfast they'd discussed the possibility of holographic "stealthing." If the Baldies could project false images, they might be able to hide themselves from plain sight. He also watched for any revealing gleams or glitters.

As they dragged their boat up onto the shingle and covered it with a layer of seaweed, nothing was in evidence but birds and fish and flies.

Then the three separated, Ashe to investigate over the hills to the north, Kosta up the road to the city and as far as he felt safe, and Ross to try the pathway to the oracle, again as far as it was feasible to do so.

Ross set out at a quick pace, despite the steamy heat radiating from rain-washed stones scattered about. An aftershock caused him to pause, watchful. He could hear the shifting of the earth below ground; it sounded a lot like a train racing along a subway line one level below, only somehow more sinister—a grim reminder of the magma explosion building toward zero hour.

Up ahead he spotted at least two major landslides. The trail still could be picked out, but he was going to have to do some detouring.

"I can make it," he muttered, shading his eyes. "But if anyone is under those tons of mud, it's not going to be me who finds them."

He grimaced, shook his head to clear it of such thoughts, and set out at a faster pace.

Stavros and Eveleen stayed silent as the ship plied its way parallel to the cliffs, heading east. His job was to keep as close to the rocks as he could without crashing into unseen ones below the surface; hers was to use the field glasses and scan constantly for Baldies. Close as they were—sometimes she could have reached out and touched the rough rock, stippled with the remains of shells from millions of years in the past—she still felt horribly exposed.

Stavros kept the engines at low to muffle the thrumming. They glided past birds' nests and crabs scuttling over wave-washed stones, past little beaches with discolored foam and dead fish piled high from the storm surf of the night before.

Nothing disturbed them, and at last Stavros cut the engine and put down the anchor.

Eveleen, sweating profusely by now, pulled on her mask; her scuba gear was already on, in case she'd have to make a fast dive.

It was such a relief to slide into the water that Eveleen permitted herself to shut her eyes and just float for a moment. The air was already unbearably hot outside and would only get hotter.

She opened her eyes, flipped over and grabbed the sled, then looked around. Ah. The cave was still there. She pointed and tried not to let herself think about quakes and rockfalls as they arrowed down, down, as she directed Stavros along the seafloor, heading for where they had left the globe ship.

They flicked on their lamps. The water was unusually turbid, masking their vision. An occasional fish flicked in and out of view, its darting seeming nervous, furtive. The light did not penetrate in shafts, but seemed to come from everywhere, a sinister, nasty reddish color.

Eveleen swam quite close to the cliff wall before she saw it. She nearly ran into the dangerous protuberances before her lamp caught suddenly on the glitter of stone newly sheered, amid wildly waving little plants of unimaginable types, colors, and variations.

Sheered rock?

Eveleen's guts clenched as she felt her way down, down, Stavros no more than a vague silhouette nearby. She remembered about how far down the ocean floor ought to be, and so once again nearly ran into a sharp, upthrust rock.

Landslide. Her breathing sounded harsh and the sharp scent of sweat filled her mask as she flipped back and forth, hands out, lamp beam moving constantly, until she was sure.

At last she sighed and for a time floated, suspended in the warm water, like the clouds of dust particles around her. Their marker had, of course, disappeared, probably buried. So, it seemed, was the globe ship.

Stavros shaped his hands into a ball and then pointed down.

Yes, it's under the landslide, blast and damn, *Eveleen thought, pointing.* It's got to be buried under all that rock.

Stav gave a shrug and then backed the sled up and anchored it a safe distance away. He flipped back and set his hands to the topmost rock. He braced his flippers against another stone and then started pushing and shoving, pushing and shoving, bubbles exploding with furious energy from his release valve.

Eveleen swam down in two strokes, set her hands to the opposite side of the stone, and pushed with all her strength.

The stone shifted; a plume of reddish dirt billowed up, obscuring their faces. Eveleen resisted the temptation to wipe her eyes—as if that would clear her vision!—and watched in satisfaction as the rock tumbled down to the seafloor.

Again they chose a big stone, worked at loosening it, and sent it tumbling with *lazy* slowness to the seafloor. Eveleen dug at the silt beneath, sending billows out into the water.

They kept digging, tossing stones and shifting mud, finding nothing underneath but more stones, more mud, and tangles of sea creatures and plants.

When Eveleen realized that they had uncovered perhaps six feet of area, and that the seafloor was maybe six feet below that, she had to face the fact that she'd chosen the wrong place. Oh, that was, as far as she could tell, where they had left the globe ship. But it could have rolled away and then been buried, and how would they ever know?

They kept searching until the warning lights on their air packs sent them up again, empty handed.

Chapter Twenty-One

The sun, an angry-looking scarlet ball of fire, dissolved into the purple murk stretching along the western horizon, leaving Ross in thickening shadows. He had a flashlight now, along with his radio and a canteen, but—mindful of Baldies and those scavenger attackers lurking about somewhere in the hills—he didn't want to advertise his presence unless he had to.

Having found absolutely nothing on his long, hot, dangerous and thoroughly miserable climb, he now discovered he'd miscalculated how long it would take to climb down.

The trail was all but obliterated. He'd had to pick his way up shifting rubble and shale, twice setting off minor slides.

Getting down was far more difficult than he'd surmised. He'd counted on following his own tracks, but the tremors after he'd started up must have set off more minor rock slides, because his prints vanished with irritating frequency.

He paused, wiping gritty sweat from his face, and stared out at the horizon. The sun was gone, leaving a faintly glowing purple bruise smearing the west, its faint glow reflected in the ocean, vanishing swiftly.

Overhead, clouds of dust and smoke obscured the starlight; the pre-Kameni Island was smoking steadily now, preparing for the next, and biggest, blast.

Meanwhile the strange, violet light would totally vanish very soon.

Get moving.

He forced himself to clamber down, glad at least he didn't have to do this climb in sandals tied on with thin leather thongs. *That's right; think of the positive,* he told himself with sour humor. Well, he'd found no bodies, except for a goat. The poor beast at least hadn't suffered; a bouncing stone appeared to have broken its neck before it knew what hit it.

No bodies, no sign of anything human. *Not that people of the past were given to litter on the scale of modern times,* he thought as he leaped over a flat stone precariously balanced on two others and came down on sand. He slipped a little, caught his balance, and sneezed from the ever-present dust. He'd had to resort to the breathing mask higher up, because of dust and smoke, a lethal combination; now its particulate filters desperately needed changing.

No, no sign of anything, animal, human—or Kayu. And what about those guys, anyway?

His question, of course, winged out into the universe unanswered, but he'd already forgotten it when he realized that the faint lights groping about down to the left were not hallucinatory flickers due to exhaustion, hunger, and miserable heat, but they were actual lights.

The landscape had changed so much he had only a general sense of his bearings. Straight ahead was the peninsula, thrusting directly west. That meant Akrotiri was to the left, though of course there were no more buildings jutting squarely up, forming a skyline.

Ross crossed a cliff face, picking his way with care mostly by feel, not by sight, until he was maybe a thousand yards above the northern end of the town. Yes. Lights. Was it his team? Should he radio?

No. If they were chasing someone, they wouldn't want to respond and give away their position. Meanwhile, he wasn't moving fast enough to get away from his own.

So he started to run, awkwardly leaping and sliding downward, until some unseen flaw in the rubble brought him down hard.

He sat up, wincing. Nothing wrenched, nothing broken—thanks to countless drills with Eveleen on how to fall without breaking your neck.

Lights again.

He filled his lungs, ready to yell, but caution made him blow the air out again and frown into the murky darkness that had so quickly descended. Yellow light, very faint yellow light. The distances weren't right for those to be flashlight beams.

Therefore... lamps?

Ah. He spotted a sturdy outcropping of ancient volcanic rock, exposed now by the ground around it having slid down toward the city.

He eased down and crept on hands and knees along that rock, staring downward, into where he'd seen those lights. He heard noises: running feet, a grunt. Fighting?

Was it Ashe and Kosta?

Linnea?

Again he filled his lungs to yell, but then a ferocious blue-white light lanced out of nowhere and for a moment lit the entire scene before it vanished.

Ross sat back, stunned by the light, by what he'd seen. The afterimage played itself against his retinas: the two obviously male silhouettes, one short, stocky, with a wild beard, the other thin and wiry, the first with a knife upraised—the blue-white light gleaming on greenish, unpolished bronze—the other clutching an armful of loot, and then the one with the knife falling, soundlessly, burned by the laser-strike.

Desperate scrabbling sounds skittered up the rock face, echoing slightly against the few still-standing walls below. That would be the second figure, trying to make off with its loot.

Those hill scavengers! But who did the shooting?

Baldies. They were here, just below.

Ross realized he was sitting exposed on this cliff and eased back slowly, looking around. Of course he wouldn't see them. What snoop gear did they have to make searches comfortable and easy? Infrared? Something that detected life-forms? He cursed soundlessly as he eased back and back, away from the cliff, and then ghosted down the side of the great slab of rock.

He was just reaching for his radio to fire off a signal—*Baldies here*—when a voice rose, an angry shout, not in Greek but in the local language.

A moment later again one of those white lights lanced out. Ross heard a thud. It was close—no more than fifty yards—and then silence.

He removed his fingers from the radio at his belt and faded as quietly as he could to the north, away from the ruins. The Baldies, or whoever had those weapons, were obviously on the prowl, and there was more than one.

He'd get to firm ground, preferably with a hill between him and those weapons, and then signal.

Chapter Twenty-Two

Linnea woke up slowly and reluctantly. Her mouth felt dry and nasty; her joints were stiff; her clothing was impossibly gritty. She felt her scalp prickle, as if all the mud in it had decided to come to life, sprouting many legs.

Is this how human beings always felt before the blessings of running water? Except that the Kallistans had had running water. She thought of that chamber in the priestesses' building, the slightly sulfuric, mineral smell of pure spring water running across stone, and swallowed convulsively.

Did she hear it?

She opened her eyes. Women sat around the rocky chamber in groups. The cell was lit, she realized. Sunlight? Was there a way out?

She sat up, looked around, saw only heavy rock, smoothed unnaturally. *Probably by some terrible laser weapon*, she thought. The light seemed to be sourceless; at least she could not pinpoint a direction in the more roughly carved, uneven ceiling, nor were there shadows to give her a direction.

She rubbed her hands over her face and listened. Below the soft murmurs of female voices she made out an almost subliminal hiss.

"Ah." Ela turned Linnea's way. "The priestess from Kemt has awakened. We feared you took injury, as did Stella." She indicated one who sat against a wall, nursing what was obviously a broken arm.

"Is there water?" Linnea's voice came out a frog croak.

Ela gave her a small smile. "It is through there."

Linnea turned around. She'd had her back to a narrow crevasse. Rising to her feet, she dusted her robe as best she could, and then made her way to the crevasse. She eased through what had once been a wider opening, but was now partially blocked by squares of fallen stone, and then stepped down into what had been a bath chamber.

Running water indeed! A stream had been diverted into two forks; one ran freely down a carved gutter, the other ran beneath a row of stone seats. She was able to relieve herself and then kneel down at the running stream and dip her hands into the water. It was surprisingly warm, and it did not look particularly clear. Her tongue dried in her mouth; she used the water to rinse her face and hands, and then got up. Would she be forced to drink that water? Would thirst finally drive her to it?

Her mind, relieved of immediate cares, fled back in memory, and she realized they were prisoners of the Baldies.

The Baldies—aliens.

Shock smote her. There had been no records of Baldies three thousand years up the time-line. Not that there were many records in Linear A... but from what she'd seen, it was mostly merchants who kept track of goods and sales with writing. Histories were orally passed down, to be written much later.

But nowhere had there been any vases painted with slim bald men in strange one-piece suits. So news of the Baldies did not make it to Crete... did that mean that these women, and Linnea, would die here?

I must do something. I must think.

She pushed her way back into the main chamber, to be met by Ela again. "The priests gave us this water," she said. "It is good to drink. It does not taste of dust, like the water in the bath chamber." She pointed to a row of three tall jugs, with several of the shallow Greek cups called *kylixes* set neatly next to them.

Thirsty as she was, Linnea paused in the act of pouring water. "Priests?" she asked.

Ela nodded once. "You did not see them, then? We are here. Priests will not let us go; we do not know yet why not. Perhaps they serve the Fire God, who is at war with the Earth Goddess."

"Did they tell you that?" Linnea asked with caution, and finished pouring her water.

"Oh no. They said only 'Water to drink' and shut this door again. It is a strange door, one we cannot open." Ela touched the smooth stone.

Linnea drank greedily and then sighed, frowning at that door. The jugs and kylixes were appropriate to the time, but that door, sliding into a tightly lasered seam, was not. Well, but when the volcano let go, there would be no evidence of this room.

Was that a sentence of death, or not?

She drank again.

Coolness spread thorugh her. She lifted the jug again, looked Ela's way. No one dissuaded her, so she drank another full cup.

Priests. Of course. The Baldies all looked more or less the same, and so the priestesses would define their strange appearance within their own perception of the world. *World.* Linnea sat down on the rocky floor and wearily contemplated the word. Did these people even have the concept of a global community in their language? Not likely.

Linnea leaned her head back. *That means,* she thought with a faint bubbling of hope inside the pit of her stomach, *that there's a chance I might just live through this mess and get back home.*

Home. She thought longingly of her clean bathroom, fresh towels, microwave, stove, her closet full of clothes, her children within reach of the phone, at least hypothetically.

Her children.

What would the Project tell them if something happened? "Your mother was blown up by a volcano three thousand years ago." No, they probably had some smooth way of handling these things. "There was an accident at an archaeological dig, far from hospital services..."

Linnea's mind drifted into depressing scenarios: her children finding out she was dead, her house empty—

Stop that.

She sat up, shaking her head. Defeatist mental whining would get her exactly nowhere. All right then, what was the situation? All she knew for certain was that the Baldies had led them to this chamber, wherever it was, and shut them in. They had given them water, and the Kallistan version of plumbing was in the chamber adjacent. That argued for a certain level of humane treatment.

That's all I know. So what do they know? They know that they have a number of Priestesses of the Serpent. They do *not* know that I am not one of the priestesses, or surely they would have separated me and used me to try to get at the other Time Agents.

Are the others even alive?

Linnea shook her head again. That, too, was unknowable. So what she did know was that she was the only one who had enough awareness of futuristic tech to be on the watch for ways of escape. If she stayed near that door, for example, maybe she'd see how they controlled it. She might see something outside the door that could help them. She might hear something—

The door opened with a low, soft hiss. Linnea looked up, startled, but before she could move, a Baldy slid in a tray. She saw the being's oval-shaped head, the fine skin with a tracery of blue veins under it, reminding her for an unsettling moment of a newborn baby's. Then the being pointed at the nearest priestess, a young woman who stepped back. The Baldy gestured.

The woman did not move.

Linnea's hands rose to her mouth as the Baldy stepped forward, plucked the woman's brightly colored linen sleeve, and drew her forward.

The door slid shut.

"Eat," said the seer. "We shall need our strength."

No one spoke. Several women crowded round the tray, softly exclaiming.

Ela brought the tray to the seer, who sat against the wall opposite from Linnea. All the women stood respectfully back as the old woman touched the stack of flat ceramic dishes, a single round container—a Kallistan jug with lilies painted on the side—the line of flat spoons. Linnea did a rapid count: nine plates and spoons, eight women now in the chamber.

There was one for the woman who had been taken out.

"It appears to be a meal," the seer said in her old, tremulous voice, looking into the container. "It is so finely milled!"

A younger woman turned to Linnea. "Have you such things in Kemt? Or is this priest food?"

Linnea opened her mouth to speak of worlds, aliens, foods that might or might not suit the human digestive system and hesitated. *Your only weapon is your brain,* she told herself. *Use it.* Were the Baldies watching to see if one of the women might be a ringer?

"It is unfamiliar to me," Linnea said only.

"I shall sample it," said the seer. She gave a wry smile. "I am the oldest and the closest to the world of the shades."

So saying she dipped a finger into the serving bowl, tasted. Presently she looked about. "It is a strange food, of a flavor I cannot name, but I do not feel the fires of poison within me."

She signed to the priestess who usually supervised meals, and in silence she served out nine equal portions.

Linnea took hers, waiting until the women had chanted their blessing over the food. Then she tasted it. The consistency was much like pancake batter, the taste not much different. She had no doubt that it was both clean and reasonably nutritious.

"It is not unlike the meal we make with fava seeds, but what herbs set thereto?" someone wondered.

Other comments were offered. Linnea said nothing; the food made her feel energy flowing back into mind and body.

She had just set aside her plate and spoon when a deep rumbling noise caused all the women to go silent, still.

The shaking started then, at first easy, then harder, great jerks and jumps that eventually died away. Fine silt sifted down from new cracks in the ceiling.

Linnea drew in an unsteady breath.

The women began to talk again in low voices, and finally the seer motioned them over, and they began to chant, a steady, soothing rhythm. In their own way, the women were trying to solve the problem, Linnea realized.

The seer shut her eyes and began her breathing.

Linnea shut her own eyes; she no longer felt superior to these women, uneducated and superstitious as they were. She just felt an added sense of responsibility: she could not sleep until she knew what had happened to the woman taken out.

Rescue, she thought bleakly, *is obviously up to me.*

How?

⚜ ⚜ ⚜

"If Linnea is still alive, she's probably not alone," Ashe said.

Eveleen felt excitement surge through her. "That mysterious room Linnea found that one day, do you remember? I really think the elevator shaft connecting the globe ship's original cave connected to that room. Do you think Linnea might be imprisoned there?"

Everyone turned Kosta's way; he was the one who had searched the ruined city.

"If she is, there's no access I can see," he said. "That entire level of the city has fallen. Not one of those buildings has been left standing. I can't speak for any underground chambers, of course."

"The Baldies obviously didn't want anyone around there, not with the shootings," Ashe said. "But they might have been trying to protect themselves against the hill scavengers."

"One of those scavenger guys was about to jump another," Ross pointed out. He made a wry face. "Though I find it hard to believe the Baldies shot the guy with the knife out of some weird sense of justice."

Ashe shook his head. "More likely he found something of theirs while looting."

They were all sitting in the boat directly under a cliff, so that they could not be seen except from the cliffs directly overhead. They'd met at dawn, as planned, rowing back under a sky streaked with brownish-stained clouds, the sea an ominous green.

Now they finished breakfast. Eveleen, glancing at the others, thought that they looked as weary as she felt.

"I found nothing on the northern shore except collapsed huts and landslides," Ashe said presently. "Ross found nothing but landslides up the mountain. I think, therefore, we should confine tonight's search to the city."

"All right with me," Ross said, drumming his fingers on the ship's rail.

Eveleen swallowed. "I would really like to search for Linnea," she said.

Stavros glanced up. He was busy with a welter of wires and plastic; Eveleen saw dark smudges under his eyes. He had not slept at all for over thirty-six hours. "I am trying here to rig some kind of a location device, using the strain meters," he said. "If we use their tech, we give ourselves away." He shrugged, his mouth tight.

Kosta sat back, his hands cradling his coffee mug. "I did not cover all the areas I would have liked. With all of us working, perhaps we can either identify sections to focus on, or else rule out the area entirely."

"What about the Kayu?" Eveleen asked. "Ought we to look for them—for rescue, if for nothing else?"

Ashe sighed. "The only location we know of for them is on top of the mountain. We'll have to assume they have taken care of themselves. We definitely can assume that they are, for whatever reason, incommunicado."

No one spoke.

Ashe nodded once. "Then all five of us will search the city area tonight, and cover it as closely as we can. We'll use infrared scanners, and a new set of radio codes. Get some sleep: as soon as the sun sets we'll outline our specific search goals, and we'll land under cover of night."

Chapter Twenty-Three

Night. Far in the north, lightning pricked the sea; the delayed rumble of thunder stayed in the distance, no more than a low, fretful threat. The air was thick with dust, still, and hot. It smelled of burned rock to Ross, who occasionally spared a glance to that storm moving eastward. It did not seem that the edge of it would brush Kalliste. Too bad. Getting soaked would be a relief.

Ross turned his head and made out Eveleen's silhouette against the soft light of the southern stars, just barely visible through the slowly drifting haze of volcanic steam and smoke.

Ross glanced down at the infrared reader in his hand. He held it out, moving horizontally from left to right. Then, when distant lightning briefly lit the rubble around him, he moved forward another thirty feet.

Slight scrabbling sounds to his right indicated that Eveleen, too, was performing a sweep-and-move.

Ross and Eveleen spent another immeasurable time working across the landscape in a rough zigzag. They could not see Ashe, Kosta, or Stavros, but Ross sensed them strung out along the face of the mountain.

So far, no one had used the radio. Could the Baldies sense them?

No sign. The infrared reader showed blurps and blobs that had to belong to birds or small animals. Some moved in hops; others jetted upward.

Sweep, pause, move. It became a pattern, almost a drill. Ross, tired from too many nights of interrupted (or skipped) sleep, was just feeling his brain settle into a kind of routine when he became aware of noise to the left.

He whipped up the reader, and at first saw nothing. But he heard harsh breathing and rubble clattering.

Lightning flared. Ross smelled the attacker a split second before he saw the stocky figure with something upraised, a sharp, nasty smell of unwashed body and badly cured goat skin. The attacker vaulted around the side of a massive slab of stone, which explained the lack of a reading.

Grunting with effort, the man heaved something directly at Ross's head. He sidestepped, and a huge jar smashed down where he'd been. The scavenger uttered a low growl and flung himself onto Ross.

An angry, desperate battle ensued, the two men teetering on loose rubble, each trying to get a purchase. The scavenger was short but enormously strong, fighting to kill; Ross was still in self-defense mode, which flared, quick as the distant lightning, when a second attacker appeared behind, a stone upraised.

Then came a sound not unlike the whirring of a great owl's wings, and Eveleen leaped up, turning midair, using her velocity to arc out her foot in a perfect side-kick. The edge of her shoe caught the second guy right across the bridge of his nose, and he howled, dropping the stone, and then launched himself at her, arms swinging.

Ross's adversary made the mistake of turning his head to see. Ross used an ankle-sweep to knock him off balance, and two solid punches, one to the face and one to the gut, sent the man crashing down the hill amid a shower of little rocks.

A palm-heel strike to the solar plexus from Eveleen sent the second one to his knees, fighting miserably for breath.

Ross picked up his infrared scanner. His heart raced, his hands trembled, but all his senses were heightened; in a weak, easterly flare of lightning he made out maybe six others, all converging.

"It's a gang," he whispered to Eveleen.

She nodded—he sensed it rather than saw it—and pulled her weapon, holding it in her hand as they eased back down to the south.

They dodged round a broken building and crouched down beside a well, both peering out, their scanners up. By these they watched the gang's progress to the southwest, downhill. Shouts, thuds, and the clatter of stones broke the summer stillness at one point.

By the faint reflected glare of the dim LED light on the scanner, Ross saw Eveleen grimace. "Took care of their two guys, is my guess."

Ross nodded. Her tone in "took care" made it clear that she didn't believe any more than he did that the scavengers dealt out first aid. Well, he had no sympathy, none at all; he flexed his hand, feeling tingles run up his arm to his neck. Probably broke a couple fingers, damn it all. Jammed, anyway.

They waited until the scavengers had moved southward in a clump; then Ross radioed the signal for DANGER: MOVING SOUTH.

He clicked off the radio and he and Eveleen scooted straight uphill, scanners constantly moving.

The rubble altered abruptly from treacherous landslides to jumbles of jutting stone, forcing them to proceed slowly.

"Something's going on," Eveleen breathed, barely loud enough to hear.

Ross saw her facing southeast. He held up his scanner. Indeterminate flickers registered on the very edge. Whatever was going on was on the other side of the ruined city.

Smash! A shower of stones and a scrabbling noise caused Eveleen to gasp. Ross crouched, weapon up.

"Na-a-a-ah!" A very bad-tempered goat plunged right between them, head low, horns butting the air.

The animal leaped, struggled for purchase, and then trotted downhill, scolding the night.

Eveleen breathed a laugh of relief. "I guess we must have stumbled onto its hiding place."

Ross risked a quick glimpse from his flashlight, shielding it with his palm. Sure enough, there was a pocket cave underneath a great fallen wall. Again, the stone was too thick for the infrared to have sensed the animal.

Ross sighed. "You know, this is a waste of time. Unless our targets are right on the surface, we're not going to get anything; these sensors just don't have the penetration we need."

Eveleen nodded. Ross saw her profile outlined against the slightly softer darkness of the sea, the water touched with reflected glimmers of starlight.

"Hear that?" she murmured.

Ross turned his head. Faint echoes of shouts rose from somewhere toward the coastline.

"Let's go see if they need help," she suggested.

"Right."

Their progress was slow, until they found a relatively undisturbed stretch of pathway. But then that, too, ended abruptly at another great landslide. They picked their way over carefully, forced to test every step, lest they be carried downhill with another slide, some two hundred yards.

But just before dawn eased the darkness to a faint, orange-tinged smear, they found the others, all except Kosta.

Ross said, "Scavengers are roaming around in a gang."

Ashe nodded. "They clearly think this city is their territory. We had to fight them off twice. Kosta went chasing after them," he added. "I searched a little more, until a landslide forced me back."

"Any sign of the Baldies?"

"Nothing found, though I thought at one point that I saw an artificial light."

"Was it just a lamp?" Ross asked.

Ashe shrugged, a gesture that looked to Eveleen almost Gallic. For some reason it made her smile. "Landslide, and then a fight, prevented us from going up there. Maybe it's nothing."

"Nothing on our end, either," Eveleen said. "Except a crabby goat."

Ashe breathed a short laugh, and then the swift crunch of footsteps brought all them alert and ready.

They relaxed when the strengthening light shone on Kosta's tired face, his stubble pronounced. He grinned.

"Find the Baldy hideout?" Ross asked.

"No. These scavengers—" Kosta shook his head, muttered in Greek, then forced himself to say in English, "After they tangled with us, several of them retreated in one direction."

Ashe rasped his hand over his chin. "So you followed them?"

Kosta's white teeth gleamed in the morning light. "Yes. And I discovered they have a ship."

Chapter Twenty-Four

"Three journeys of the sun."

Linnea sighed, trying to rest her aching head. There was no rest, not in a chamber made of stone, with only a thin blanket of some synthetic material for cushion.

How absurd, she thought restlessly. As if the seer could distinguish such irrelevant matters as day and night. "The battle will begin in three journeys of the sun." That's what she'd said, and that's what the priestesses believed.

They also apparently believed that the priests kept them here for some grand purpose, because in their culture, no one maltreated the oracle or her Sisters of the Serpent. And Linnea could not bring herself to shake the old woman and scream, "Wake up! These are aliens who hate human beings, and you're just mouthing out a lot of superstitious nonsense that will be nothing but matters for scholars of antiquity and children's comic books in my time!"

But she couldn't. She could see herself doing it—felt the words forming behind her lips, her hands aching to grab and shake, and then she could envision the result: hurt, anger perhaps, but above all, flat disbelief.

They were sure the priests were kindly people, if strange, because so far, none of the women had been hurt.

The first one had returned after an immeasurable time, to speak of being given a beautiful cloth woven of wondrous stuff that had moon – and starlight threaded through.

And when she wore the priestly garment, why, she could hear the inner voices of the priests, just as if she were a seer!

The others had listened in fascination as the priestess described how the "priests" invited her to talk about her life, and about what the seer saw and when she saw it, and how the people responded. At first it was difficult to shape the words in her head, but she learned to do it, and finally they took away the priestly cloth, and she no longer heard the spirit voices, and they brought her back.

Linnea, feeling sicker by the moment, translated that into real terms: the Baldies had thrown one of their shimmery blue cloths over her, which enabled them to hear the thoughts of the wearer, and the wearer to hear theirs. One of those blue suits had nearly cost Ross Murdock his life, when he first became a Time Agent.

Another woman had been taken, this one gone a much shorter time. Then another, but after her, they had not taken a fourth for a very long time.

The fourth had just disappeared; the women, unafraid, now had chosen among themselves who would go next to visit the spirit voices.

Linnea could not tell them why she would resist as long as possible. She would not tell the priestesses who she was because they wouldn't believe her. But revealing her real identity to the Baldies, who would believe her, would put not just her in danger, but also the priestesses and the Time Agents.

She glanced at the women now. The one with the broken arm was asleep but moaning softly. The seer was also asleep, a faint snore escaping her open mouth. The others sat, either meditating or talking in low voices so as not to disturb the sleepers.

All right, *Linnea thought.* So that means I have to do something—

A tremor seized them, and the women went silent, looking up. Yes, more silt drifted down, and more cracks appeared overhead, and especially in the walls. Two in the floor. In the far chamber, Linnea heard the water splashing up over the rock, just like her children used to splash water out of the tub when they played, lunging from side to side to make waves.

She frowned at the crack. The quakes were more frequent now, and Linnea thought they were getting steadily more violent, though that might just be her fear, that and the widening of the cracks.

"Oh, her fever worsens." A voice penetrated Linnea's thoughts.

At once several women crowded around the one with the broken arm. Linnea edged near, glancing down. The others had set the arm, as far as she could tell, well enough, and had wrapped it in strips torn from their robes.

The woman cried, and then turned her head away in shame, biting her lip, as Ela carefully unwrapped the last layer, exposing purple dotted flesh. Linnea's guts churned as she stared at the swollen skin, the greenish tone. Infection. The bone had probably shattered, and there was no way of knowing whether or not the setting had gotten it all back together, or not. But one thing for certain: major infection had set in.

Linnea backed away, moved to the front for one of the empty cups stacked neatly for the next appearance of the Baldies, and took the top cup. Useless worrying about who drank from which: germs were not even remotely in this worldview.

Linnea ran to the far chamber and dipped the cup into the running water. It, too, was running turbid, probably carrying dust and debris from the latest quake. Couldn't be helped.

With her back firmly turned to the crevasse that gave access, Linnea dug under her robe for her pouch. Down at the bottom was the plastic packet of super-powerful antibiotics that the Project doctor had issued each Time Agent. She pulled open the package, pulled out one of her four pills, and crumbled it into the cup, stirring with her finger.

Then she set the cup down to permit the drug to finish dissolving, and stashed the rest of the medicine in her pocket. She straightened her robe, her mind running through explanations: just as she was unwilling to thrust a modern view of hopelessness onto these women, even less was she willing to pose as a miracle worker.

She picked up the cup, stirred it once more with her finger, and then carried it carefully into the other room.

"I have herbs from Kemt," she said.

The others all looked up at her. She realized she had become isolated from them. Not ignored, precisely, but because she did not participate in their rituals, or their conversations, she had closed herself in with her thoughts, and they had slowly closed her out of their awareness.

Now several pairs of dark eyes, all expressive of hope, tracked the cup she carried. Ela helped the sick woman raise her head as Linnea murmured, "It is bitter. But all must be drunk."

The seer, who had woken, smiled very faintly. "Are not all herbs bitter?"

The sick woman sipped, winced, and then, at Ela's soft murmur in the unknown tongue, drank the antibiotic-laced water very quickly, leaving nothing but a trace of powdery, chalky-looking residue at the bottom.

"I shall save it," Ela murmured, pointing. "Stella can drink it later, if this eases the fire within her."

Linnea nodded, backed away, and then the door opened, and the absent priestess came back in.

She smiled. "It is just as you say! Spirits speak when you wear the priest cloth. They are very powerful priests, and very blessed, it would seem."

The seer turned to face Linnea. "There is only me, and Stella, and she is so ill." The old woman narrowed her eyes. Her expression was impossible to interpret, but it seemed to Linnea that she was doing her best to descry some sign from Linnea. "Shall you go, then?"

Linnea shook her head once. "It is not my time, Maestra," she said, hoping she sounded oracular, and not merely sulky—or sinister.

But the seer only bowed her head in acquiescence, and slowly walked through the open doorway.

Linnea could not see the Baldy outside, but she sensed its presence.

The door closed.

Chapter Twenty-Five

Night again.
Or what seemed to be night.

When Eveleen woke up, her sinuses clogged, her mouth dry, she sat up blearily. The late afternoon light was weird orange. The sky was covered with what looked like gray rubble: a mixture of cloud and smoke that appeared dirty and threatening.

A faint whiff of civilization resolved into fresh, steaming coffee. A mug pressed into her fingers, and she sipped, her eyes closed.

When she opened them, Ross was hunkered down on the deck next to her hammock, looking like a movie-land wild man with his long, curling hair bound back by a bandana, his fatigues, and his fake-fur pouch still worn around his waist. He had no shirt on. None of the men wore shirts; the weather was oppressively hot and still. Eveleen resolved mentally that, if she couldn't rightly go shirtless, she could at least make her thin robe work for her instead of against: she would soak it thoroughly with water before she did anything else. Her scalp, too.

"When we get done," Ross began, and Eveleen mentally added the "if" that Ross would never say out loud, "they're gonna owe us a paid vacation. A big one. Where do you want to go? Paris? San Francisco, where it's foggy and cool?"

"I want to go to a spa and soak for a week," Eveleen said.

"I want a prime-rib dinner," Ross said, "and all night to eat it."

Eveleen cudgeled her aching brain to top that, but the urge to be silly for a blessed time was all too brief: there was Gordon Ashe, patiently waiting for them to finish. He didn't interrupt, or frown. He simply sat on his hammock, half a sandwich in his hand, his expression blank.

Ross glanced up at his chief, gave a sour smile, and said, "More good news?"

Ashe shook his head. "No news. Kosta took off at about ten this morning. Went down to find that globe ship. Said he thought about it all last night, and insisted he knew just where to look."

Eveleen shook her head. "Isn't he ever going to sleep?"

Ashe quirked his lips in a grim semblance of a smile. "He said he'll either sleep for eternity, if we're caught here, or else he'll sleep for a week when we get safely home, but either way he won't get any rest running around on top of a fifty-thousand-megaton bomb that stinks of burning rotten eggs."

Eveleen laughed, then got to her feet. "Who can resist a call to arms like that?"

As she spoke, she studied Ashe. He'd lost that restless, angry nervousness she'd sensed earlier, and he seemed to have come to some sort of decision. Not that anyone could really read him, of course, but she lingered for a moment or two, waiting to hear how that decision would translate out into a plan.

After a little more chat about the technicalities of the dive, she said, "Well, I'll get cleaned up and ready, if you'll tell us what's next."

"I don't know," Ashe replied. "Depends on what Kosta comes up with—"

"Here he is, if I'm not mistaken," Ross said, poking his head up through the hatchway.

A lot of splashing and some gasped curses in Modern Greek resolved into a dripping Kosta.

Everyone swarmed up on the deck, waiting in silence as he pulled his breathing mask off. He blinked away sweat, then said, "It's gone."

Eveleen, stunned, said, "The globe ship?"

Kosta glanced her way. "I shifted the rest of that debris we found. It's gone."

Ross let out an expletive that seemed to sum up everyone's feelings.

"Gone like taken?" Ashe asked.

Kosta shook his head, dropping down wearily onto a bench. "It's buried, so deep it's impossible to get to." He looked up at Eveleen. "I believe there was not just a massive landslide, but a fissure of some sort opened, the ship fell into it, and a slide occurred. The landscape down there changed, some of it shifting about twenty yards west, and then dropping."

Everyone looked stunned, considering what that meant.

"Well," said Ross, "at least that means the Baldies can't get to it, either. I hope."

"We'll have to make certain," Ashe said. "But not yet. Everyone get ready: we'll meet back here in ten minutes. First we search, and then we'll plan further."

Eveleen went down to the sweatbox. As she untangled the sweaty mass of her hair, she yanked impatiently at one of her earrings, as usual caught in a mat. The other wasn't, for once; she felt, and then jerked her face up to the tiny mirror.

The other earring wasn't caught; it was gone.

She touched the hole, saw a tiny scab, and vaguely remembered a sting there during the fight the night before. So she *had* lost an earring in Akrotiri! She'd lost the earring—but was still alive. So far... She grimaced, knowing that up the line in the future, she and her remaining earring might still be buried elsewhere.

"It's not a good sign, or a bad," she whispered to the shower. But would anyone else, such as Ross, take it badly?

She hustled through a quick semblance of a cleanup and dressed, her mind racing. When she stepped out, she quietly removed the other earring and stowed it with her gear. There. Either it, and she, made it back, or they... didn't.

Then she straightened up, refusing to think about it anymore. But that was no comfort. Her mind promptly reverted to Ashe and that look of resolve, of a decision having been reached. Whatever Ashe's decision had been, he hadn't shared.

Or was she just imagining things?

She got one of the dried-looking sandwiches that Stav had put out and sat down to wait for the others.

A strong quake sent the surf crashing out and then in again in strong waves, nearly sinking their rowboat.

Once again the entire team was there.

No one quite wanted to say it, but this was their last search for Linnea. The silent testimony to the north lit the sky like a vision of hell: the plume of smoke from the preKameni Island had widened gradually into a wide, glowing red. Between wind-torn flaws in the smoke they could see veins of lava shooting up into the sky.

They were far too close to the point of no return, and they still did not know for certain that the main controls to the devices were on the globe ship. Ugly as the sky looked, the constant quakes might still bleed off just enough energy to prevent the great eruption if the Baldies could reactivate their devices.

One more search for Linnea, then, and after that, they had to put all their effort into finding out if the Baldies' tech was elsewhere besides the missing globe ship.

Meanwhile, their boat floated, unguarded, at anchor, its only protection a crumbling cliff.

They rode a mini-tsunami that deposited their rowboat high on the beach. They landed with a jarring smack. At least it was above the fly-covered sea wrack. Ross could smell the rotting fish and seaweed, and he could hear the buzzing of great clouds of flies, but at least he didn't have to see the revolting mess.

He helped the others drag the rowboat up farther, and then they did their best to camouflage it with a reed mat.

After that came the grueling climb to where Ashe had seen the light. This time, the last time, they would all look.

Ross bided his time as the others began walking. When his wife fell into low-voiced conversation with Kosta about the scavengers' ship, Ross took a long step and fetched up next to Ashe.

In the dim red glow from the north, Ashe looked grim but amused. "And your objection is...?"

"I haven't known you all these years not to smell a dead rat when the stink hits me," Ross said.

Ashe breathed a soft laugh.

"You're going to find those damn Baldies and offer to trade yourself for that woman, aren't you?"

"What makes you think that?"

"The fact that you didn't outline it as a possible plan—one that you know we'd all veto. I'll bet you Linnea Edel would, too, if she were listening in."

Ashe shook his head. "I should not have let her come. This mission was not the right one for a beginner, and—" He paused, looked north, then said only, "I owe it to her children to send their mother back alive."

They're grown up, Ross wanted to say, but he knew it would sound wrong. Just because he'd been abandoned at an early age, had never had a family bond, didn't mean it didn't exist for other people. He'd learned that much from marriage.

So he said, "You don't know that she's alive, or that they have her."

"No. But it makes sense that they'd take hostages, if she were alive. After all, we got their ship—we had it—and time is running out."

"But we still don't really know that the globe ship vanished. They could possibly have gotten it back. We still don't know if there's another ship, or not. Maybe there is, with high-tech recovery equipment. Or maybe they've solved the exclusion principle and can slip back in time, get it, and then move it somehow."

"Or maybe they don't have it," Ashe retorted. "It could be so buried they can't get at it. All I know is, if I find them and we can't break her out any other way, then I have to try."

There's going to be another way, Ross resolved, tightening his hand on his weapon. *Watch me find it.*

When at last they came for Linnea, it was almost an anticlimax.

The seer had returned, peaceful in her conviction that she spoke with spirits through the blue priests. They had said that when they finished talking to the women, they would send them on their way.

"Stella cannot take her turn," the seer said, looking down at the sick woman. "And yet the priests need to bring us all before their spirits. But there is still this problem, that time is short."

Moral suasion, then. The seer wouldn't tell Linnea to go, but it was clear that she, and all of them, except the sleeping Stella, expected her to go. Linnea looked at the expectant faces, the innocent trust there, and bit her lip hard.

She heard the step of the Baldy behind her.

She filed out behind the alien, knowing that she could do nothing else, as the seer stood looking down at the woman who slept peacefully for the first time since she'd broken her arm.

Chapter Twenty-Six

*H**ere it is,* Linnea thought, trying to walk steadily on legs that trembled. She gripped her hands beneath her robe, sidling her eyes here and there. *Should I run? But then they will know I'm a ringer before anything else happens. The others did not run.* And besides, her knees were so watery she was afraid she wouldn't make it five steps.

Well, *she thought, trying to steel herself,* then I must think only in the old language, and *be* a priestess from Kemt, just as Gordon told me to be.

That conversation on the road to the oracle now seems a hundred years ago, she thought sadly as she followed the silent Baldy up a rough rock corridor.

At least the walk was not long, just around a rough stone corridor into another room, a small one, with plain local furnishings and a jumble of unrecognizable objects on a central table made of olive wood.

Behind the table waited several Baldies, one holding an armful of shimmering blue-green cloth. "Baldies." Now that she was face to face with them, the old nickname seemed more inappropriate than ever. Not that they weren't bald; they were, indeed, hairless, at least in terms of what was visible, and the absence of eyebrows and even eyelashes made their faces very hard to read.

Yet she made out individual characteristics as one held out the cloth, shook it slightly, and then cast it over her head. One whose light-colored eyes were wider spaced than the others, another with a narrower jaw, one whose ears protruded, just a bit.

A hole had been slit into the fabric, through which her head emerged. As the cool weight settled on her shoulders, she held her breath, trying hard to think in complete sentences in Egyptian, but when the telepathic augmentation opened a sense she had never known she possessed, she gasped, staring around.

Wonder and delight and fear flashed like silver eels amid the stream of tumbled images and words that, she realized with an internal wail, were all in English.

Mentally she reached, trying to snatch it all back, but of course her thoughts were gone, as thoughts do vanish, only this time she felt the stream wash over her listeners, for their reactions in turn splashed back on her.

No anger, no leaps to kill, no growls of vengeance—that much was clear but little else. Outside of surprise, their reactions were too complex for her to comprehend.

A whisper of communication, too quick for her to catch, zapped among all the Baldies.

They, in turn, caught the word *Baldies* from her. Again, she knew this from their reaction and from the riffle of humor that streamed through her mind and vanished, but afterward she sensed recognition, the assembling of clues, and the name *Ross Murdoch*. To which she, inadvertently, responded with a vivid mental image.

Another exchange between the Baldies, even faster than the previous; all she perceived this time was relief, a sense of "at last!" and then resolve, as if an order had been given and received somewhere else.

And then one "spoke"—if shaping words into sentences and sending them by thought can be termed speaking. In English, of course.

You are another from the hidden Time.

The mental images with the words were fast flickers, well controlled: a very young Ross, wearing a dirty blue-green outfit, launching across a fire at someone; what looked like a laser battle around a great globe ship; men speaking Russian; and some other images that she could not identify, but which she guessed were other Time Agents, encountered in prehistory.

Linnea perceived the statement not as a question but as an interrogative, and she braced herself. They already had her identity, and probably her purpose, and of course they held her life: what had she to lose?

She frowned, trying to shape her emotions into clear sentences, when quick and facile as a swift in the sky came the thought: *Say it aloud, if you like.*

"Why are you forcing your way into my mind? Why not just talk to me, since I'm already here as a prisoner?"

It is that your words and the motivations and meanings behind them so often contradict. And with those words came the unsettling sense of being made dizzy, as if trying to listen to two conversations at once, or to watch two scenes at once.

"All right, then. As for my own time, let me say this, too, and you'll 'hear' it as truth: I resent being kept a prisoner," she stated. "On my own planet. I, and the others, came back to this time to save our civilization. Our actions are those of rescue, not destruction. Can you possibly say the same?"

Yes, said the Baldy with the narrow jaw. He (she realized she chose "he" as a default, though there were no signs of gender that he could perceive, other than the slender shoulders being somewhat broader than slender hips; again, she felt a riffle of humor, but no information, from them) spoke aloud.

We must protect the galaxy's diversity of life. Only that way can it attain the full consciousness that is its goal and its flowering. With the words came images, many of them incomprehensible to Linnea. But from them she identified a problem that was very real in her own time: the extinction of hundreds or thousands of species by a technological race.

What you do on your own world is not for us to decide. But we will not permit you to do it to other worlds.

Linnea was discovering that their mind voices were individual, too.

Another Baldy, somewhat taller than the others, mind-spoke in cooler terms: We seek the minimum interference that will prevent you from developing space flight until you are mature enough not to want it, or not to misuse it, *the alien said.* We do not destroy worlds. As ours was.

And with the words came images of possibilities, what the Baldies could have done, such as destroying Australopithecus with a tailored plague, or sending asteroids to detonate in Earth's atmosphere.

But beneath the explanation—and they waited for her to perceive it—lay the specific memories of these specific individuals: arriving in their own time, not distant from the now of Kalliste and its volcano, to find that their own sun had been detonated.

She saw, and felt, their reaction of shock, disbelief, terror, grief, anger, all emotions human enough to strike deeply into her heart.

"Who?" she shaped the thought, and the reply was an echo from them all:

The Kayu."

❧ ❧ ❧

Here," Gordon Ashe said, pointing.

Eveleen paused, wiped her stinging eyes, and surveyed the scene. It looked more alien than the alien landscapes she had visited in her travels away from Earth: rubble, fragments of jars painted with stylized seed pods, stacked reed-matting beds, and all around landslides, lit by the glowing-coal smolder from the north.

It was the glimpse of dancing monkeys that snapped the puzzle pieces together, altering the scene from unfamiliar to familiar, just as Kosta said, "I remembered those monkeys. It was about here last night that I felt the need to turn away, turn back, and I heard you being attacked." He pointed at Ashe. "And so I ran down that way." He indicated the darkness to the south, toward the harbor.

"I know where this is," Eveleen breathed. "It's that square we told you about. The one with the weird compulsion."

Ross, who had been slowly circling the rubble, looking high and low, paused, hands on his hips, looking back. "I feel it," he said in a short voice.

They all stepped toward the rubble-surrounded walls of the square house. At once Eveleen felt that inner tightening of danger, and she could see, even in the ruddy dim light, that the others were tensing up.

Ross stepped up next to Ashe. His voice was low, but his wife, attuned to his moods, to the softest utterances of his voice, heard him breathe: "Remember what I said."

Ashe did not react. He motioned to the others. "Here's what we do."

⚜ ⚜ ⚜

Linnea gasped. "The Kayu? Who are they? Some kind of futuristic super-villains?" Though the Baldies had said those words about conflicting meaning and statement earlier on, she wondered if it was the seeming-truth of the master liar: if she were being manipulated not just through words, but mentally.

"They believe in noninterference."

"Blowing up a sun is not noninterference," Linnea answered back, before the Baldies could organize and send to her the mental images that they wished to accompany their words.

You must wait, *one responded mentally.* You cannot communicate with our speed in this way, and you are forming false understandings.

Linnea paused and received a series of images: the Kayu with their furry appearances and their warm robes, creatures of a very cold world, an old world. Not all thought alike, as one would expect from a race that did not share a common mental plane, but they did believe in leaving life to progress as it would toward eventual reunification in Telos.

Telos? Linnea thought, fighting for comprehension. That simply meant "goal" in Greek, but underlying the word were feelings or images of light and energy and awesome power. Were they talking about the Big Bang? Or the Big Crunch at the end of time? Everything was coming far too fast, though she could feel the Baldies' efforts to slow down, to keep their images simple.

"When they discovered that we had learned how to travel across time as well as distance, they began to follow. They are here now, having perceived across several centuries our efforts on this island."

Linnea struggled now not to comprehend the *what* but the *when*. Of all the tenses in English, the future perfect progressive is the most clumsy: "by [future date] we will have been making..." Now she realized that the Baldies could not possibly share their language, that they had several modes and conditionals within that single tense that she couldn't understand any more than she understood quantum physics.

"Most of our people are gone, except those who were on missions," the Baldy stated. "Many do not know yet what has occurred at home. We are here to complete our mission because it would guarantee a peaceful world here. And when you do reach space, you will not go as a plague."

"We are also here to find Kayu and eradicate them, that our time might restore our world," another said.

But we do not know which of their individuals carried out that mission; many of the others are also travelers like you, and have been forbidden to interfere except by truthful exchange of information.

Linnea struggled, and struggled, and finally burst out, "When is your time? Is it now? Is it in my time? Is it beyond my time? Because if it's not beyond my time, how do you know that our world takes destruction to the stars? And if it is..." She faltered in a welter of conditional verbs.

"The time-line we give to you with our interference here does not kill a whole people," the Baldy stated. *It gives your world a future of peace.*

"But it also takes me out of it, or if I were stuck here, it takes my children out of it," Linnea said, fighting against tears. But they clogged her throat anyway, making her voice quiver like an old woman's and her eyes sting and blur, so that the Baldies became mere forms standing before her. "My children have a right to their existence. Everyone who is born has a right to existence, everyone, including you. I am sorry for your world, but don't destroy mine. My children want to make a better world, as do all the people I know and value—"

It was right then that the sizzling crackle of laser fire sheered into the doorway.

The Baldies turned as one, their mouths open in consternation. Swiftly they withdrew in the other direction, leaving Linnea standing there.

She heard a shout. "Linnea! Are you in there?"

It was Ashe.

She moved to rip the cloth from over her head, but paused. The Baldies were disappearing, some of them taking some oddments she realized hazily must be part of their technology.

Dark figures entered, bringing a sharp smell of smoke and sweat and hot, burning metal. Lasers lanced out again, not at anything living, but at the few bits of Baldy tech left in the room.

She slapped her hands over her eyes, bewildered, confused, but above all desperate for answers. She flung out the mental cry: *You talked about my time and time now but not our future time. Which future is it?*

No answer.

Are you us?

No answer.

Then someone pulled the cloth from her head and flung it away, and the world slammed round her again, imprisoning her thoughts inside her skull.

She was still standing there, her hands over her face, and tears smearing down her palms, when she heard Eveleen's soothing voice: "It's okay. We're here now. The Baldies hightailed. They can't do anything to you."

Chapter Twenty-Seven

"It's going to blow!"

Who shouted that? Eveleen couldn't tell; the roar of groaning, cracking rock was louder than the biggest thunderstorm she had ever experienced.

The violent red glow all across the northern horizon had visibly increased during the short time they'd stormed the Baldy hideout.

Eveleen watched Ross gape at it and then force his eyes away. She knew what he was thinking: he would deal with what it meant later. Right now, that spectacular lava fountain cast enough light for them to see by.

They began picking their way down the landslide. Ross and Eveleen had just reached a wall and were about to vault it when Stav let out a shout and raised his weapon.

All of them stopped, ready. Down the trail from them was a cluster of figures. But the figures turned, none of them yelling or fighting, and in the weird red light they recognized that they were all women.

Linnea Edel gave a gasp. "The priestesses! They have let them go."

"We've got to get them off the island," Ashe stated.

Yes, but how? Eveleen had an unpleasant inward vision of their ship crowded with women who belonged in a world three thousand years in the past, but then Kosta smacked his hands together. "The scavengers' ship."

Ashe grinned. His teeth glinted in the bloody light.

"We might have to scuffle for it," Ross warned.

"Then all four of us can go," Ashe said. "The scavengers can see to themselves. These women deserve a chance to get away from the blow, but if they don't do it soon, they might not make it." He turned to Eveleen. "You get them some supplies off our ship. Stuff they'll understand," he added. And to Linnea, "I take it you know how to communicate with them?"

She nodded.

"Then explain that they need to get going, now, fast, either south to Crete, or if they're afraid of missing the island, then northwest to Greece. Anywhere but east."

She nodded again, and started speaking to the women.

Eveleen, after the first few sentences, stopped listening. Linnea was talking in Kallistan terms, making it all simple. Eveleen realized that the preparations for food would be entirely up to her; time was running out, and she'd better hurry.

When Linnea paused, Eveleen whispered, "I'm going to run ahead and row myself to our ship. Take them to the beach and wait. We have radio," she added. "Here. Take mine. If I need to, I'll contact you with a spare from the ship. If the guys beep a signal, beep back four quick ones, which is the emergency code." She sighed. "At this point, I suspect Gordon will break silence and come on in the clear and talk to you."

The older woman looked tired and worn in the terrible red light. Her eyes were puffy, but her gaze was alert and focused. "All right," she said in a soft voice. "I will meet you on the beach, then."

Eveleen ran the rest of the way down, or rather slid, skipped, hopped, and once rolled. Even with the roll—a painful one, over what seemed to be every pointy stone on the island—she was glad to be going down, not up. The air was hotter than ever and filled with smoke that smelled of hot rock.

She found the rowboat, cast off the covering, and was about to jump in it when two figures emerged from the shadows under an outcropping of rock.

A guttural-sounding roar from one gave her enough advance warning that this was no friend and to pull out her weapon. She aimed at his feet and fired.

Hot, smoking sand blasted up.

"Ow!"

A gargling howl of anger from the other presaged a berserker attack. She jerked up the weapon, realized she still couldn't bring herself to fire, and reversed it, dodging the flying fist that came at her head, and pistoled the man across the mastoid bone. He went down like a felled tree, stinking of years-old sweat, stale wine, and uncured goat skin.

Gagging, she turned around to deal with the second one, to see him running westward down the beach, his pumping legs flinging sand up behind him.

Using her breathing techniques, she tried to calm her jangled nerves and forced her watery legs to function as she shoved the rowboat down to the water.

Having learned the hard way about rowing, she wrapped some old seaweed around her palms before picking up the oars. A few good, hard pulls, and she launched into choppy waves. The water looked as black as ink, except for the oily reflections of the distant lava shining an unpleasant red in spilled ripples of color.

She reached the boat, guided by a faintly glowing buoy bobbing around in the water, tied the rowboat to the stern, and clambered aboard.

There, she hesitated. For the past few days they'd moved the boat right into the harbor at sunset, trusting to darkness to hide it, and then they'd returned to their little cove, sheltered by crumbling cliffs, at dawn.

But Linnea had clear orders, and she couldn't see to execute them without lights.

Maybe the danger is over, she thought, and went ahead and turned on the lights. Not the ones she knew would light the deck, if needed, just the ones below.

Then, trusting to the murk outside to hide any cracks of light, she got busy.

Linnea forced herself to concentrate on walking, which was a challenge perilous enough. The terrible red light from the north was bright enough to distract one but not bright enough to highlight the many places on the walk down where the foot could get stuck in a hole or cause one to slide.

The priestesses had given Eveleen mildly curious looks, though in the darkness her mixture of modern clothing (khaki trousers) and Kallistan (her knee-length thin linen robe) had barely been visible. Linnea did not worry. She knew by now that what you expect to see you see. The priestesses were not looking for visitors from the future any more than they had recognized the Baldies as beings from another world.

Their only conversation was about the strangeness of the blue priests. Between the time Linnea had been taken away and their subsequent freeing, they had managed to convince themselves that the priests had sought someone from Kemt.

"Perhaps," Ela said as they trod in single file, except for the two helping Stella, "they wish to go there, as our island is where the spirits have chosen to battle."

"Yes," several of the other women said.

"Our island is no longer a place for the living." The seer's old, cracked voice was wry.

Stella stumbled; the other two caught her up but necessarily jarred her arm. She gave a hiss of pain but made no protest. The others fell silent, the youngest two smoothing the road with their sandaled feet so that Stella would not trip.

In this manner they made their way slowly down to the beach. Out on the water, Linnea saw a tiny row of golden lights. That had to be their ship. She felt a surge of relief at the idea of settling down into her hammock once again.

The others exclaimed in mild voices and then sat down above the line of sea wrack to wait. Linnea was thus left alone with her thoughts, which arrowed straight back to her conversation with the Baldies.

What could she think? Her mind reeled with questions, with emotional responses to the questions, and of course no answers. She longed to sit down with Gordon, except she suspected he would have as few real answers as she did. He'd fought against the Baldies but did not know them.

Were they the enemy—or not?

She was just wondering when the sound of shouting voices carried, faint as the cry of distant seabirds, from the ruined city behind. She turned. The priestesses all turned. The thick, still air carried the sharpness of male shouts but no words.

Then, out of the darkness lanced three or four bright blue points of light. They arced across the ruins, and one angled down past the cliff at the water, hitting the boat!

Their boat!

She sank down onto the sand and covered her eyes.

Chapter Twenty-Eight

The men had just climbed, dripping, aboard the scavenger ship when they saw lights lance out of the darkness, pierce the thick smoke obscuring the sky, and then stab across the harbor.

Ross squinted against the eternal haze. He saw a brief, reddish flare of burning wood. Their ship! Someone had blasted their ship!

He grabbed the field glasses away from Stav, cursing steadily as he slammed them to his eyes. Eveleen was on that ship...

But when he brought it into focus, he saw a shadowy figure moving around on the deck. It had to be his wife. Or...?

"Come on, let's move," he snapped.

"No wind. We'll have to use the oars," Kosta replied.

Ashe was at the other side, watching the ruins through his glasses. Stav, Ross, and Kosta each picked up oars. Ross was glad that the galley wasn't belowdecks; the surface of the deck stank bad enough. Whoever those scavengers were, it was abundantly clear that basic hygiene was not remotely a part of their paradigm.

At last Ashe closed up his glasses and sat down to pick up his oar. He matched rhythm with the others, and then said, "It's difficult to be sure, but I believe the scavengers regrouped and tried to rush the Baldies."

Kosta said, "They might have been drawn by the noise we made in our raid."

"It's possible," Ashe said. "It's also possible that the Baldies think they're part of our group, or that we're allied."

Stav snorted. "They might not even know the difference."

Ross sighed, trying not to worry about Eveleen. "I wonder what the hell they did, or said, to Linnea."

"I expect we shall soon find out," Gordon said, and then they fell silent, putting their backs into lift, push, lift, push.

The scavenger ship had a very light draft and skimmed along the water, which was alive with little waves. *Nervous little waves*, Ross thought. The sort you'd expect to see after a whole lot of earthquakes.

They rounded the last point and angled in toward the harbor. Out on the water, which reflected glitters of crimson from the increasing glow northward, they perceived a small black lump.

Ross's heart gave a lift when the lump resolved into a rowboat with a single occupant: Eveleen.

As they drew abreast of the figures waiting on the shoreline, Kosta sounded the bottom with his oar. They maneuvered in as close as they could, and there followed a couple hours of very hard work.

It was especially hard in that murderous light, with the possibility of being fired upon by more weapons. No one knew where the Baldies were, or why they'd fired, or where the scavenger gang was, for that matter. So they worked as quickly as they could, helping Eveleen unload the barrels of water and the sacks of grain and beans and lentils that she'd selected for the priestesses.

"You're giving away all our camouflage," Ross whispered to his wife as they passed the sacks up into the scavenger ship.

She snickered. Then said, "If we need camouflage anymore, then we're in serious trouble."

Ashe gave them a grim smile as he passed up a big hard round of goat cheese that Kosta had traded for in the harbor the day before the big quake.

"I put some purifier in the water," Eveleen added in a murmur. "It might not last their entire journey, but I figure their systems have to be used to whatever biota will develop by the time they reach Crete."

"That's the last barrel," Ashe said. "Let's get them aboard."

Among those on the first trip was a woman whose family had been fisher folk. She understood the basic principles underlying hauling wind. Through Linnea (the women did not talk directly to men, they discovered, though Ross noticed a couple of the younger ones taking peeps at the four male Time Agents, Kosta and Stav especially), Kosta gave some quick lessons.

The woman nodded, obviously listening carefully. She seemed to comprehend that their lives were in her hands.

Ashe said, at the end, "Tell her that it's important not to go anywhere east."

Linnea looked up. "We discussed it while we rowed over. She says she'll take them northwest, if the gods of the winds will smile on them. It's easier to find land than it is to find islands."

"A wise choice," Ashe said.

All this in Ancient Greek, of course.

Ross and Ashe then bent to help the last woman up, the one with the broken arm. They waited while Linnea gave her a cup of something to drink that she said was more Kemtish herbs. From the bitter smell, Ross guessed she was dosing the woman with antibiotics. Good idea.

And then they climbed down, the five of them balancing in the little rowboat. Linnea crouched down into a ball in the stern sheets, and off they went.

Ross watched the women take control of their new home. Some of them were already cleaning, throwing garbage and filth over the side, others busy settling the sick one. The pilot was handling the sail as if she knew what she was doing, and the narrow little craft picked up speed, sailing away westward on the faint, fitful breeze stirring off the water.

I hope they get away, Ross thought, and then turned his attention back to the others.

"I think it's safe to talk," Ashe said, as the oars lifted and splashed. "Our boat first. What happened?"

"I don't know," Eveleen replied. Ross could hear her regret and self-blame in her voice. "I turned on the lights below in order to see what I was doing. Did that make us a target? I didn't think the light carried."

"I could see tiny pinpoints of light," Linnea murmured.

Ashe said, "The contrast with the total darkness in the south was apparently enough to guide their aim. Did you see how much damage was done?"

"No, I just turned on the fire extinguisher, and left the foam all over, then got back to the last of the flour sacks. I didn't know what else to do, outside of getting that food to Linnea's group," Eveleen replied.

Various nods of acquiescence from the others were the only response.

Ashe said, "Linnea? Are you ready to brief us on your experiences? Or do you require some recovery time?"

"No, I can talk," the woman said. She sounded at first as if she'd aged ten years, but as she spoke her voice gained firmness.

As Linnea outlined what had happened to her, they finished crossing to the ship.

Kosta was the first one up. He dashed below, then returned, and in the reddish light from behind them, Ross and the others saw his relief.

They didn't nail the engine, then, Ross thought, and sat down on deck. The air was miserably hot, smelled worse than ever, and faint sounds, a rushing rumble, emanated from the distance. Hairs prickled on the back of his neck. Yeah, they'd said a whole week, but his body thrummed with fight-or-flight adrenaline. It sensed danger now.

"...and that is when you came in," Linnea finished. "I was not able to ask any more questions, nor clarify any of theirs to me."

Ashe rubbed his hands over his face.

Ross said, "Well, look on the bright side. At least we fritzed out any tech they had there. I shot it all myself. So they can't come after us, especially if the globe ship is gone."

While the others talked, Eveleen and Stav went down to the little galley area, and the homey smell of freshly ground coffee added its blessed, and unlikely, scent to the terrible odors of a volcano preparing to blast.

Kosta had gone down again to clear away the mess that Eveleen had made with the extinguisher foam and repair any holes he found.

So it was Linnea who looked from one to another, and at last back to Gordon Ashe, before saying, "It changes everything, does it not, if it's true?"

Ashe sighed. "I think we might take it as true. Let me brief you, and you tell me what you think."

So he told her what the Kayu had said and recounted everything else that had occurred since she'd gone. He also told her what the big quake was, how it had been set off.

She pressed her knuckles against her mouth once or twice but otherwise stayed silent.

When Ashe was done, her first question took Ross by surprise. "Did they say they had somehow monitored the Priestesses of the Serpent? Perhaps radioed suggestions to them, as part of their policy?"

"They didn't say anything like that, but it's not out of the realm of the possible," Ashe admitted. "Why?"

"It's just so strange that the seer predicted that quake just before it happened, sending the people to evacuate. And you say that most of the city had gotten out of the buildings and down to the shore before it struck. That is an astounding coincidence, if the Kayu, or even the Baldies, were not manipulating the priestesses without their knowing."

Ashe stirred as Eveleen and Stav passed out mugs. For a time no one spoke, and the only sounds were those of the water lapping against the sides of their boat, the creak of wood in hull and mast, the distant, harsh cry of seabirds, and farther off that hydraulic whumble that promised violent action soon.

Then Ashe said, "I really believe that those questions are, for now, academic. The thought I cannot get away from is that we're going to have to go back up into that ruined city and rescue the Baldies."

"What?" Ross nearly dropped his coffee.

"Huh?' Eveleen stopped in the act of pouring more.

Stav said something under his breath, and down below, Kosta cursed in Greek.

Only Linnea nodded, a slow nod. She'd expected just that, Ross realized. "It changes everything, doesn't it?" she said. "That they have a ... a moral directive? Each of them? The Kayu saw behind the Baldies' mandate a genocidal logic, and killed their sun in order to save other worlds, and the Baldies were changing worlds in order to protect some future that we are not permitted to see, lest we change it even from here and somehow destroy our fulfillment?"

Ashe laughed. "You put it better than I would have. I was going to say, 'Damn it; it's the right thing to do.' "

"But they shot at us! They shot at our boat!" Ross protested.

Linnea looked his way. "But we don't know that. Did you not all agree that the Baldies might not be able to tell the difference between you and the scavengers? That it's possible they thought this boat theirs?"

"What a nasty judgment on us," Eveleen muttered. "Not to see a difference."

"Yet that could have been true all along," Ashe said. "We've encountered them in the past. We don't know if different groups of them are ones who've just discovered their murdered world or if they've mixed us up with people of our prehistory, but either way, we probably haven't looked too good to them."

"Is this rescue plan a voting thing, or not?" Ross asked.

Ashe turned his way. "Do you think we need to vote on it?"

"No, I think we need to act, and fast. I don't care what the Kayu said about having a week. That damn island in the north is blowing bigger by the minute. If we're going in, let's go and get the hell out. Remember, where we're sitting is part of the caldera."

Ashe nodded. "Let's get in, then, and do what we must."

He turned to direct Kosta to start the engines, but then the radios at everyone's belts gave a brief, high burst of static and then lit.

Ross and the others grabbed their radios.

From them, in wide-spectrum stereo, came the mellifluous voice of the Kayu translation computer. "We shall take the !!! with us. But departure must be immediate, if you are to successfully translate both space and time."

The seabirds shrieked, unheeding, and the water lapped against the sides, a subtly faster pattern. The only human sound was Kosta's voice, still cursing.

"The seven days we spoke of was predicated on certain energy figures at the time, but those have considerably altered," the voice went on. "There is no safety here for finite beings; only the entity can remain. You must go, and so shall both our races, the !!! having failed to destroy your time-line and we having failed to hear the entity we sensed cross time."

"Entity?" Ashe said, looking puzzled.

"The entity that only the serpent woman could sometimes hear. And it would not speak when the !!! placed their devices in the temporal world."

"Wait," Linnea said, taking Ashe's radio from his hand and kneeling on the deck to speak into it. "Tell us! What have we done in our future to make them so desperate to destroy us in our time?"

There was no answer.

Ross realized that Kosta's cursing had gotten louder.

Ashe said, "Kosta? The engines?"

"Are fine," Kosta called.

"Then fire them up and get us out of here. Unless there's another problem?"

Everyone now got to his or her feet, crowding around the hatchway.

Kosta stood there looking up, his face gleaming with a sheen of sweat, his eyes black, his mouth tight with anger and tension.

Stav gasped, and said something in Greek. Kosta shrugged one shoulder and then said, "The onboard damage is not too bad, just some splinters and melted plastic—but the time-gate is compromised."

"Compromised? How?" Eveleen asked.

"The Baldies' laser fire damaged the portal rods. If we can't fix them in time we won't be able to sync up with the gate."

He gestured at the violence behind them. "And then we shall see, up close, Kalliste become Thera—"

He stopped, but they all knew what came next: *before we die.*

Chapter Twenty-Nine

Fear. Eveleen stood there on the deck, trying to think.

The mission was over. They were done. In fact, they had to leave. But the time-gate was broken.

None of these facts caused the least reaction in her. She felt unreal, as if the red sky and the black sea and the never-ending smell of burning rock had replaced reality.

Her eyes turned Ross's way. In the ugly red light he, too, looked stunned.

Then Gordon Ashe moved. "Let's get down to the fixed point as fast as we can; we have spare rods." A rattling roar from the disintegrating island punctuated his words.

Stav shook his head. "Yes, we shall, but it will be a close thing. And even with the new rods, can we recalibrate it well enough in the time we have left?"

"What does that mean?" came a whisper at Eveleen's shoulder. Eveleen cast back a distracted look and saw Linnea.

"All speed. Set the sail to help," Ashe added, as the wind had been flowing out of the west—and they knew that the wind would carry the volcanic detritus east—but no sailing ship could sail into the eye of the wind. Bracing the sail round to catch that west wind might aid the struggling motors and help propel them southward just a bit faster.

Eveleen said to Linnea, "Whether or not we manage to fix our side of the time-gate, we still have to get to the same spot the Russians are waiting at." She paused. "Good news and bad news: it's probably close enough to reach before the volcano blows but too close to survive if the gate fails us."

"But what did Stavros mean about recalibration?" Linnea asked.

"Our signal, which emanates from the portal rods, allows the Russians to calibrate the gate at their end. I don't understand the details, but the science types all agree that it's dangerous to linger when passing through a time-gate—and no one knows, or wants to know, what happens if you try to back up. There's some indication that that's what happened to a big Russian time-base that blew up a while back. At the time we thought it was the Baldies. Now—"

Linnea nodded. "So passing through on a boat sounds dangerous."

Eveleen nodded. "The scientists were afraid of that, so they put those engines in so we could get through at what they figured was a safe speed. But now, if the Russians don't get an accurate reading and open the gate at the wrong moment, well, I suppose the resulting bang will be lost in the Thera explosion, but we won't know."

Linnea winced.

Ross and Stavros were already busy at the simple sheet-ropes and braces that controlled the single sail. And there was a breeze, if a fitful one, stirred by the hot air coming south meeting the western flow. The water currents were also fitful, probably due to steam vents opening in the ground below the sea.

As Linnea watched, the men finished sheeting the sail home, and the ship began to pick up life. She realized she could not hear the engine adding its contribution to their speed; she could only feel its vibration.

"Now," Ashe said, his voice rasping with evident exhaustion. "Konstantin. Tell us what to do to help fix that timegate, if you can."

"We must generate light on deck," the man replied, making motions with his hands. "I must disassemble the rods and lay out the pieces so that I can examine the damage."

"That's a clear order," Eveleen murmured. "Our part is to clean up the deck, then." She sent a humorous look Linnea's way, hoping to ease the woman's stricken expression.

Linnea nodded, gave her a perfunctory smile, but it was a polite smile, and did not mask the inner turmoil that Eveleen could so plainly see.

They worked quickly, and in silence, shifting all the decorative "trade goods" belowdecks—those that they'd gotten for the scientists, that is. The fake things they threw over the side, figuring every bit that lightened the boat's load increased speed. And in the blast to come, no one was ever going to find those floating plastic jars or fake furs.

The blast to come—maybe it had even started. Eveleen saw that she was not the only one glancing often over her shoulder at the north. The scary thing was, they didn't seem to be moving at all, yet she was able to feel the wind and saw little rippling waves slapping up the bow and passing, with oily looking foam, down the sides. The current did not seem to be setting north, so what was the problem?

When they got the last items clear, and the men began bringing up the big metal rods that were the frame of their time-gate, she stood on the taffrail and stared northward.

No, the familiar outline of Kalliste had diminished. But what had steadily grown was that red glare in the north. In fact, it had grown so much that it seemed to have come closer; the red now climbed high into the sky, tentacles of glowing smoke straining toward the horizon. Dawn was near: a greater light glowed in the east, but underneath it spread the violent reddish-brown cloud, reaching horribly outward in snaking fingers. Some even stretched westward, writhing upward like a monster out of the worst nightmare. Eveleen made out house-size chunks of matter spewing high into the sky and coming down with fiery force into the sea.

The sound, she realized, had grown steadily, a rumbling, rushing roar.

"It's as I thought," Kosta said.

Eveleen turned around and saw that he had laid out the portal rods on the deck. She'd thought of them, from the name, as being simple rods of metal; instead, they were hollow cylinders, now open like elongated clam shells and packed with circuitry and bizarre metallic shapes.

"The shunts in several rods were overloaded somehow by the Baldy weapons. I suspect they actually are a combination of laser and plasma fire, carrying quite an electrical punch."

"Did we pack enough replacements?" Ashe asked in an equally loud voice, his tone superficially calm, but there was a hard snap to his consonants, the question that is not quite an order.

"Of course, a full set," Stav shouted. "More than we need."

Everyone heard that, and Eveleen saw the hope in their faces.

Ashe said, "But will it take longer to replace the bad ones and test them all, or just replace them all? I assume we'll have to check the calibration of every one of them, whether or not we replace them."

"Exactly, especially under these circumstances," Stav said, after a short colloquy with Kosta during which they both glanced at the island slowly falling away behind them.

"Then let us not risk any weakened ones. Let's replace all the shunts. That, any of us can handle," Ashe said. "Stav and Kosta are the only ones who can handle the calibration; that leaves two rods for each of us remaining."

Stav nodded once and then knelt down to explain how to install the shunt cradled in his hands.

But before he could speak, a deep, ripping clap spun them all around. As they watched in horror, flame jetted upward from that distant island far into the sky, followed by a cloud of hot steam.

Moments later heat smashed at them, and the boat surged over the top of a big, warm, green wave that raced outward at unimaginable speed.

"Come on!" Ashe shouted. "Get to work!"

Eveleen saw everyone force his or her attention forward again.

They listened, with desperate focus, to Stav's explanation and demonstration—the process a simple mechanical one—and a brief systems check. Then the rest of them began work on the other rods while Stav and Kosta installed and began to calibrate the first one.

Soon there were fewer rods unrepaired than waiting, freeing some of them to assist.

Stav motioned Eveleen into the bow, where she crouched, looking back along the length of the ship. She couldn't help herself. She had never been able to turn her back on danger, and this was the worst danger she had ever confronted in her life. Thick globular shapes rose high into the morning sky, spreading out; as yet most of the eruption pushed into the east, carried by the higher streams of wind.

In those globes incandescent ash could be seen darting about like gigantic fireflies from hell.

Eveleen hoped the fleet had not gone east; any of those clouds of burning ash touching ships would convert them into instant gas.

"Is that it?" Linnea cried, working next to Eveleen, who could only shake her head. The noise pounded her ears, her skull, her teeth, her bones.

Stav appeared next to them, handing a completed rod to Linnea and motioning so they put their heads close to his. His breath smelled absurdly of coffee, Eveleen realized, which added to the surreal aspect of the terror gripping them all. One part of her gibbered in weird laughter; the other apparently took in his rapid flow of instructions, though when she looked down, her hands lay there like a pair of spiders, unconnected to her, unable to move.

"Here, help me push it down," came Linnea's urgent voice, her lips just next to Eveleen's ear. She'd already placed the portal rod in its bracket. "This one first, and then that one," she said, motioning to the wire harnesses and jacks.

Ah. This thing first and then that.

Simple directions seemed to be what she needed. Another clap, even louder than the first, caused them all to jump, but. everyone worked fast. Eveleen knew that the unmeasured tons of rock being spewed into the sky would be coming down soon, bringing with it a killing downblast that would send out lateral shock waves of volcanic glass shards to shred whatever wasn't being burned by the ash clouds.

They were running out of time...

"Next."

They moved along the hull to the next position. Linnea again settled the rod. Now Eveleen's hands worked quickly, independent of her mind; her eyes tracked Linnea's small hands, with their thin skin stretched over tendons and age spots, but fast hands, expressive hands.

Yellow light, weird yellow light, cutting weakly through the red-shot darkness slowly enveloping them, made Eveleen realize that the day had been banished by a volcanic night.

The air was hot; another surge lifted the ship, passed beneath, and set them down, bringing even hotter, thicker air, more difficult to breathe...

Someone slapped a mask over her face. She did not look up, but kept working. As she breathed in gratefully, she realized how close she had come to fainting.

But they were done. She looked up, her head pounding, her thoughts thick as the lava spewing into the stratosphere overhead.

Linnea motioned; no one could hear voices anymore. The roaring had taken over the world.

Eveleen crouched where she was as Stav, with a face of pain, reached down and triggered the gate. She looked over the side of the boat, but the sea was so frothy and filthy with ash that she couldn't tell if it was boiling along the portal rods, as it had when they had first passed through the gate. How would they know when they were synced?

A third clap, this one so loud they could only feel it as it tried to scour their bones, and Kosta smacked the engine into high. Hot wind blew into their faces as the ship shuddered, racing fast over the churning water.

Eveleen's imagination jammed into overdrive as well. As vividly as though she were somehow there, like a god proof against the violence, she saw the magma exploding upward, vaporizing the pre-Kameni Island, billions of tons of white-hot rock and searing gas punching up through the atmosphere almost to the edge of space, spreading out in a choking cloud that would bring killing winters to the Earth for years to come. And below, the sea racing in, exploding into super-pressurized steam as it raged against the liquid rock.

Another surge, the greatest one yet, raced under them; they braced for the murderous shock wave of steam that they knew would be following behind—

And air and earth and sky began to rip apart in an explosion of noise and light and power. Her bones shuddered as the night around them flared with light and ahead the strange straight-line vortex of the gate manifested, sucking in the violence rushing past them.

Eveleen felt hands seize her roughly, throwing her violently down on the deck, and Ross's body on top of her. Moments later the gunwales burst into flame sleeting violently forward under the impetus of the hell wind chasing them; the sail vanished in a flare of light and the mast burst into flaming splinters. A thunderclap smashed at her ears, clamping her skull in a vise of silence while the devil played his organ music through her bones. Eveleen squeezed her eyes shut and shouted with pain as a whip of fire flayed her and the nausea of the transition was lost in a world of pain—

—and the shaking roar ceased abruptly, the fire cooled. The boat rocked violently for a moment, then calmed.

She squirmed out from under Ross and slapped at her smoldering clothing and then at Ross's. He'd been more exposed than she. She barely noticed the pain of her burns; what she did notice was the pressure in her ears and a total absence of sound.

Around her the others did the same. It appeared that everyone had come through. They were alive.

After a moment she stood up and looked around. The still-smoldering gunwales of the boat were burnt almost to the deck; all around them, she could see sparks falling gently down upon the sea like a benediction.

Eveleen ripped off her half-burned mask, and sucked in the cold air, still tainted with the breath of hell that seemingly had tried to follow them through the gate. She wondered what it had looked like from the Russian ships, now faithfully veering in toward them.

They were alive, and *home.*

She turned her face into Ross's shoulder and wept.

Chapter Thirty

It was just over a week before Ross heard his wife's voice. Until then, he could see her lips move, and he could see her changes of expression, and feel her arms around him, but his ears seemed stuffed with cotton batting. That was all right. Cotton batting was far preferable to that head-slamming blast back in the past.

Then sounds started coming in. Their first conversation was about their hearing; Eveleen complained that a bosun's twee had been set off in her brain, and she couldn't find the off switch.

They joked; they rested aboard the unmarked ship the Project had had standing by. They slept a lot. When they were awake, doctors ministered to them, at first patching up their burns, clearing out their lungs and sinuses, prescribing food, rest, and lots of water. Ross had no arguments with that.

Milliard came in by helicopter; Ross woke up one night to the *whup-whup-whup* of the blades, which he could feel more than hear, and next morning at breakfast there was the big boss, looking like the CEO of a *Fortune 500* company, except maybe tougher.

His lips moved, but Ross couldn't hear him. So they began communicating on-line; there were terminals all over the ship.

At first Ross didn't want anything to do with their questions, with debriefing, even with remembering. But the memory will not be denied: if one fought hard enough against it all day, it popped out again at night, taking control of one's dreams with such a vengeance one awoke, sweating, thinking they were all back in Kalliste again, and the pre-Kameni Island was going up maybe a hundred yards away.

So Ross gave in, answered one or two questions, then Eveleen started sending him playful e-mails, and before he knew it he spent those soft, summery days sitting out on the deck with a keyboard in his lap, typing away.

When he could hear again, the interviews started: Milliard, Project heads from various departments, and of course the medical teams, including psychologists.

They were interviewed separately, though no one made any attempt to keep them apart. Their own hearing functioned well enough to do that, had there been any urgent need for individual testimony.

Memory gave way to thought, and thought eventually produced questions—the foremost ones fueled by anger.

It was some time after the main battery of interviews was over that the entire group found themselves sitting out on the deck under an awning. All around them the sky softly wept, clear, clean rain, sky, air, and sea all a silvery gray.

The gentle drumming of raindrops on the roof merely served to make it seem warmer somehow underneath, as they helped themselves to a fresh pot of coffee brought out by the steward.

Gordon Ashe sat forward and gave them what Ross recognized as his scan look. "So, any thoughts?" he asked, sipping coffee.

They obviously weren't going to hear his thoughts first. Ross had no problem with that. He had no problem with leading off, either.

"I'll tell you what fries my butt," he said.

Linnea Edel's eyes crinkled. Kosta grinned his pirate grin. "What's yours?" he asked.

Ross laughed. "You too, huh? Well, mine is this: those damn Kayu guys had the gall to judge us! I mean, look at it. They came on the radio like that, without us connecting in or anything. They obviously were listening to every stinking word we said while we sweated out those last few days. Every word. So they only speak up and tip us the clue that the whole damn island was about to blow *after* Gordon got his harebrained idea of rescuing the Baldies."

"That makes you mad?" Eveleen said, her brown eyes going round.

"Of course it makes me mad! That they could set themselves up in judgment like that, without letting us know. And if what the Baldies told Linnea is true, they don't exactly have clean hands."

"Irrelevant," Ashe said—*at his most maddening*, Ross thought with unrepentant grumpiness.

"Game playing," Kosta said. "I hate that." He grinned. "Unless I make the rules."

The others laughed, and Kosta went on, "We never perceived the rules with those ones. They had rules as far outside our ken as automobiles, computers, and TV shows are outside of the Kallistans'."

"In other words," Gordon said, "they made us feel stupid. Granted."

"Not stupid," Linnea Edel murmured, looking around at them earnestly. "Stupid is ignorant and doesn't care.

We knew we were ignorant and we did care. We cared passionately."

Murmurs of agreement rippled round the group as the rain kept drumming overhead and far in the distance gulls screeched. *It is good to be home, in our own time, if not our own place*, Ross thought, swallowing down his coffee.

Stavros spoke up, taking the others by surprise. He'd been so quiet during the mission, like many engineers, living mostly inside his head. "I want to know," he stated, his English very accented. "I want to know what is this entity to which they referred."

"So did the brain boys," Ross said. "At least during my turn on the hot seat."

Nods of agreement from everyone.

"Well, I want to know, too," Ashe said.

Ross shrugged. "I think they went nuts. I mean, don't try to tell me those guys suddenly started believing in fire gods." He snorted, reaching for the coffee pot to pour out some more. "Or do they mean there's some kind of mysterious alien force living in the volcano? Give me a break—that's almost as bad."

"One thing I learned while I was so briefly a prisoner," Linnea said in a slow voice, "is that, even if I were to have told the other women about my time, what vocabulary would I have used? These women were not stupid. They were thinking beings, aware of their world, involved, several of them wise—much wiser, I think, than I will ever be—about certain kinds of things. Yet I'd be forced to use the language of childhood to describe a pair of nylon stockings."

Eveleen nodded. "That's what I thought. *Entity* could mean almost anything, and our mistake would be to assign our old rules to it, especially old rules we automatically distrust."

"I figured it had to be another sort of alien, at first," Kosta said. "From what I understood on that last radio transmission, the 'entity' couldn't 'talk' to the oracle woman while the device was in place."

Stavros nodded. "That argues for physical limitations of a sort that we can understand."

"Unless the noncommunication was not related to physical limitations but to some other set of rules, some we can't possibly imagine," Ashe said.

"Like what? Gods playing chess with us and the Baldies?" Ross scoffed. "If you're going to start gassing about gods then I'm going back to sleep."

"I'm playing devil's advocate," Ashe said, with a faint grin. "Probably a more comfortable post, at least in today's deterministic paradigm."

Ross knew that Ashe was joking—and he was the butt. He sighed. "Look. I just don't know, and none of you do, either, about that kind of question. So why get into it, since we can't really know?"

"Because it's interesting, trying to apprehend the infinite," Linnea said. "I, too, scoffed and thought myself so superior to those poor benighted women with their snake dances and their oracle, there in the dirty cave with stuffy air. But by the end, I began to see that in certain ways, I was the ignorant savage, and not they. Their perception of the universe was clear, it had moral rightness, and for all my superiority in realizing that they couldn't see the Baldies as aliens, only as priests, how many things were around me that I could not see, that they could? There is always the chance that at least Maestra, their seer, had in some way glimpsed past the shadows on the cave wall."

"Then you think there's a fire," Ashe said, looking across at her.

"I think that there are times when we feel the heat of it and see things reflected from the light of it," she said, even more slowly than before. "Don't you?"

Ashe sat there, staring out at the open sea. "I didn't, when I was young, but now, after years of seeing strange things, unexplainable things, I can only safely admit to my own ignorance."

Eveleen said, "Well, those Kayu knew there was something there. And so did that priestess. We found out too late to make our own investigations."

"And who knows if we would have found anything? We might still be too ignorant: all our tools are the wrong tools, our questions the wrong questions, because we so often have, if unconsciously, preformed conclusions," Linnea said. "It seems to be the curse of our modern times: we think we know enough to strip the meaning from all the past paradigms, without replacing it with anything."

"And without really comprehending the underlying meaning that made those paradigms work in the first place," Ashe put in. "Well, it ought to be interesting, the future. The Kayu and Baldies both know not only where we are but *when* we are."

"Do you think they will show up here, then?" Linnea asked.

Ashe shrugged. "It wouldn't surprise me."

"But we don't really know that they are from our own future. It could be that they cannot go forward, only backward," Kosta stated.

Stavros pursed his lips. If he had thoughts about time travel and aliens, he wasn't speaking.

Ross sighed. "Back to the speculation."

"Ah, but we're so good at it," Ashe said, smiling. "Why not indulge ourselves?"

"Because to me it's running in circles. Give me a clear goal and the tools to take action, and let me at it. I hate palaver that can't go anywhere," Ross said. "If that puts me in the ignorant camp, I think I can live with it."

Linnea smiled over her coffee cup at him. "It puts you in the camp of those who act. I am in the camp of those who react. There is, I believe, a place for both."

Ashe turned to her. "Does that mean you want to stick with the Project, then? Despite a fairly harrowing first trip?"

"Oh, yes," Linnea said. "Oh, at first I thought that I would never even be able to look back, and then I started looking back, and then I thought I would only stay on to consult on others' experience—Milliard specifically invited me to do that—but these past few days, I find myself thinking of things I would do differently next time. And that means I want there to be a next time."

Eveleen grinned. "So you got bitten, too, eh?"

Linnea turned to her. "Yes. So I told the bosses that I'll go home, revisit my children, as I promised myself, but I'm going to design my life differently, I think. Even the briefest glimpses of our past are treasures, and I want to be the treasure hunter."

"She's bitten," Ashe said.

They all laughed, and presently they got up and separated, all to various tasks.

The ship would dock in two days, the bosses having decided that they had enough preliminary material and that the agents were rested, had no mystery viruses or diseases, and were due some extended leave time.

Stavros headed straight back down to the labs, where all the instruments on the boat that hadn't been broken in those last few desperate hours were being evaluated. Kosta was up on the bridge. Gordon and Linnea went off to talk to some of the archaeologists that the Project had on staff.

Ross lingered longest, standing at the rail, trying not to think, but thinking anyway. When he finished his coffee, he went down below, and sure enough, there was Eveleen, in the midst of a workout.

He waited until she was done, then said, "We did talk about what to do when we got out, but we didn't decide. Or don't you want to think about the future yet?"

Eveleen gave him a too-innocent grin. "Oh, I think we should visit Hawaii—and go tour the big volcano!"

He chased her halfway around the ship before he caught her.

About the Authors

Andre Norton was one of the best-loved and most famous science fiction and fantasy authors of all time. She was named Grand Master by the Science Fiction Writers of America and was awarded a Life Achievement Award by the World Fantasy Convention. She wrote over a hundred novels which have sold millions of copies worldwide, including her Witch World, Beast Master, Solar Queen, and Time Traders series, among others. She passed away in 2005.

http://www.andre-norton-books.com/

Sherwood Smith was a teacher for twenty years, teaching history, literature, drama, and dance. Before that she worked in the film industry for several years. She writes science fiction and fantasy for adults and young readers; she has been working on the Sartorias-deles fantasy series all her life, beginning with the CJ Notebooks, then continuing on as her main protagonists began to grow up and become active in the world.

Though known primarily as a fantasy writer, Sherwood along with author Dave Trowbridge collaborated on Exordium, a five-volume space opera, with Rachel Manija Brown on the young adult "hopeful dystopia" series called The Change, and with Andre Norton on four books listed elsewhere.

https://www.sherwoodsmith.net/

About the Publisher

This book is published on behalf of the author by the Ethan Ellenberg Literary Agency.
https://ethanellenberg.com
Email: agent@ethanellenberg.com

Made in the USA
Middletown, DE
06 November 2024

64051689R00146